Elvis and the World As It Stands

Written by
Lisa Frenkel Riddiough

Illustrated by
Olivia Chin Mueller

Amulet Books • New York

Library of Congress Cataloging-in-Publication Data

Names: Riddiough, Lisa Frenkel, author. | Mueller, Olivia Chin, illustrator.
Title: Elvis and the world as it stands / Lisa Frenkel Riddiough, Olivia Chin Mueller.
Description: New York : Amulet Books, 2021. | Audience: Ages 8 to 12 |
Summary: After being sadly brought home from the animal shelter Elvis
learns to appreciate his new family, especially ten-year-old Georgina
Pemberton who builds skyscraper buildings in her bedroom, and Elvis
realizes that both humans and animals can build a world of their own
choosing, even if the choices are not what they had initially expected.
Identifiers: LCCN 2021005887 | ISBN 9781419752391 (hardcover) | ISBN
9781419752407 (paperback) | ISBN 9781647002015 (ebook)
Subjects: CYAC: Building—Fiction. | Family life—Fiction. |
Self-reliance—Fiction. | Architecture—Fiction.
Classification: LCC PZ7.1.R535 Elv 2021 | DDC [Fic]—dc23
LC record available at https://lccn.loc.gov/2021005887

Printed and bound in U.S.A.
10 9 8 7 6 5 4 3 2 1

Amulet Books are available at special discounts when purchased
in quantity for premiums and promotions as well as fundraising or
educational use. Special editions can also be created to specification.
For details, contact specialsales@abramsbooks.com or the address below.

Amulet Books® is a registered trademark of Harry N. Abrams, Inc.

ABRAMS The Art of Books
195 Broadway, New York, NY 10007
abramsbooks.com

For James and Julia

For Georgina,
Build a world of your own choosing.
Happy 10th birthday!
Love,
Mommy and Daddy

THE BIG BOOK
OF
AMERICAN ARCHITECTURE

By Eliza Joyce

Ormond + White Publishers
San Francisco

PART 1

Chapter 1

Ah, afternoon naps! Always interrupted by Etta's prickly paws, sticking and stabbing their way from the top of my head to the tip of my calico tail.

"Hey!" I say. "You're treading in your sleep again!"

"What? Huh?" Etta says in her scratchy voice. "Elvis. Let me sleep." Such a feline.

The *click click click* of the wheels on Carly's cart echoes through the shelter. It's music to my ears, because I'm starving. And everyone knows Carly's cart means dinner.

"Etta! Wake up," I say.

I peer through the glass of our condo and watch Carly roll up to the whiteboard and look at the calendar. She grabs that stinky black pen and puts a nice big *X* in the box that marks today's date, which is, of course, Saturday, July 3. I take note of tomorrow's box, all decorated with blue-and-red starbursts. The Fourth of July Adoption Extravaganza! I stretch my paws wide up the sides of our condo door and laugh at myself as I form an X. Etta copies me.

"We're just a couple of Xes, aren't we, Elvis?" she says.

"Sure are," I say.

"Our forever family is out there waiting for us, isn't that right, Elvis?" Etta says. Her eyes sparkle when she talks.

"Indeed," I say.

"Quiet down over there," Rupert calls out from across the room. Long-haired party pooper so covered in fur it's hard to believe there are eyes in there somewhere. I don't know how that fat cat sees a thing.

"Get back to napping, Rupert," I say.

"I would if you weren't such a loud know-it-all," he says.

Then, saved by the *snap-click* of the lock on our condo door, it's Carly. With a full plate of chow.

"Hello, my sweet peas," she says.

I tell her, like I do every day, "Carly, please call me Elvis." But Carly doesn't listen. Such a human.

"I know," she says. "I love you, too."

I just shake my head, turn on my motor, and give her a nice, strong headbutt. Humans love that.

"Eat up," she says. "And, look, I've got your favorite alphabet book."

Oh good, the alphabet book. It's the best. Full of letters. Like *X*. Humans love their letters. One day I'm going to crack their code. I just wish it wasn't so hard.

Etta and I chomp and crunch at our kibble, and Carly opens her book.

"*A* is for Appreciate Art," Carly reads. Everyone knows that. Who wouldn't appreciate art? "Do you know what else *A* is for?" she asks.

I crunch my kibble and think about it, but I can't come up with anything. This is what I mean about cracking their code. I can't figure out how humans make the letters mean something. You're supposed to put them all in a row. For writing. And reading. It's tricky. But if I could get it right, I could communicate clearly. Just talking to a human never works.

"*A* is for animal adoption," Carly says. "And that's what's happening tomorrow."

I already know that. But Carly wants to keep on talking about it. She says something about new families and new homes and adjusting, but I'm waiting for her to get to the letter *B*, which stands for "Become Brave." She never gets there. Fine. I just nuzzle her a bit and smile over at Etta. We're both so excited.

"We're going to have a brand-new, wondrous life, isn't that right, Elvis?" Etta says.

"Yes, indeed," I say, with a twitch of my whiskers.

"There are no guarantees," Rupert snorts from across the room. Rupert. Please.

"What do you think our forever home will be like?" Etta asks.

"Like that one story in Carly's fairy-tale book, of course," I say. "An enormous yard with rolling hills and green grass and trees filled with blue birds and a pond with fish! The out-of-doors. The fun never ends in the out-of-doors! Oh, and the banquets of food. So much food. The best—"

"And so many blankets," Etta says. "And cushions. NEW blankets and cushions!"

"Ah, the blankets," I say. "Thick and soft and warm."

"Don't forget about the villains," Rupert says.

"Our forever home won't have any villains, will it, Elvis?" Etta says.

"Of course not," I say. Villains. Please.

Carly closes the alphabet book. "I think you are all too excited to concentrate on reading," she says. I guess she's right. The alphabet book will have to wait.

"I'm sure going to miss you," Carly says. "Good night, my sweet peas. See you tomorrow for the big day." Carly *snap-clicks* our condo door and leaves.

"When we're at our forever home, will we ever come back here?" Etta asks as she tumbles around me and tugs on my tail.

"Why would we?" I say.

"I don't know," she says. "We've lived here since the beginning. It's not our forever home, but it's our home, right?"

"No. No," I say. "It's just a shelter."

She nibbles on my tail, and we swat at each other and laugh.

"You don't know anything," Rupert says. Poor guy. If only he knew that he's the one who doesn't know anything.

The place quiets down, and it's lights off and motors on.

Etta and I get to grooming.

I start at my tail and work my way through my calico colors. Mango, ebony, cream, and rust. One in a million. That's what Carly says about me. *Etta and Elvis*, she says. *The original American Idols.* I spend quite a bit of time working on the tufts of my paws. There's something there I can't quite get at, so I bite and pull. Got it! A clump of kitty litter. Please.

Etta helps me a little, and I help her, too. Eventually she tucks her head into my neck and treads. The pushing and pulling. The grabbing of tufts of fur. I wouldn't trade it for anything! Her rumble is soft and sweet.

The gray of her tummy rises and falls with each breath. The tips of her little white paws twitch and snap. She's dreaming of our forever home. The mother, the father, the children. Maybe one of those very old humans. Yes, a grandparent. And friends visiting. And naps. Wonderful naps.

I close my eyes and sigh. It's a dream come true. Etta and me. Together forever. In our forever home.

The Fourth of July Adoption Extravaganza can't get here fast enough.

Saturday, July 3, 7:12 PM

Good evening, G.

Hi Daddy!

What did you do today?

Worked on the Sears Tower.

Wow! Great work!

Remember when you and me and Mommy went to Chicago?

There's a pic on ur phone. Please send.

Will do.

Give me a minute on that.

Don't forget, 4th of July BBQ tomorrow.

Mommy is dropping you off at 9AM.

Yay! 😊

I love you! 🖤

I 🖤 U 2

 # Chapter 2

New day. Same prickly paws on my backside reminding me that this is my life. I can't help but smile.

I clear the morning fuzz from my vision and see Carly standing right in front of our condo.

"Good morning, my sweet peas. Rise and shine. We're moving you up front to a condo in the spotlight," she says.

Before I even have time to consider this, Carly opens the door with a *snap-click* and grabs me by the scruff. She tucks me under her arm and grabs Etta, who is just waking up.

"What's happening, Elvis?" Etta says.

"We get to go to a new condo today. For the big event!" I say.

"Oh! Wow!"

Carly walks us down the corridor—felines on the

right, canines on the left. The corridor is cool and musty, just the way I like it. I fill my lungs.

I consider wriggling out of Carly's grasp to scoot off on an adventure, but with the adoption extravaganza coming up, who has time? Also, those awful mutts are snarling and snapping like they own the place, and I don't want to accidentally cross their paths.

The Second Chance Club comes into view—those poor, hopeful souls. They're injured and old, and some of them went to their forever homes but got returned. They're supposed to get a second chance, but Rupert calls it the You Don't Stand a Chance Club.

Ah, there's the front desk, up by the double doors of the entrance, with the cardboard carriers stacked to the ceiling. I grin at the posters on the brick walls. Pictures of happy felines sitting in confident poses. They'll probably take our picture, too, when Etta and I get our forever family.

Carly deposits us in our new condo up front. It smells fresh. Nose-tingling clean. I twitch my whiskers and sniff around. From here, I can see everything in the whole shelter. There are red, white, and blue sparkles everywhere. And flags, too. With stars and stripes. There's one on every condo, next to our identification cards. I try to fiddle with the one on ours, but I can't get to it from inside the condo.

"Elvis!" Etta says. "It's the Fourth of July Adoption Extravaganza!"

"Sure is," I say.

Rupert lands in the condo next to ours. "I preferred the back room," he says.

"But this is the place to be if you want a forever home," I say.

"Forever is too long for me," he says. "And I don't need Old Glory, either."

"You're the old one," I say.

"It's the name of the flag," he says.

"I know," I say. Of course I know. I'm not stupid. Please.

Carly checks our water bowl and gives us some breakfast. "I'm so happy for you two," she says. "Look! They're all in line at the front door."

Etta and I turn toward the front desk and the doors beyond. The humans are crowded outside. There's a whole pile of miniature humans, too, jumping up and down and tugging on their parents like a litter of puppies. It's a little overwhelming, but they look happy and special, like I knew they would. They can't wait to meet us.

One of the volunteers opens the doors, and the crowd pushes its way inside. My ears twitch with all the screeching. A tiny human rushes up to our condo and bangs on the door so loudly that I jump and hit my head on the ceiling. Etta crouches in the corner.

The dogs bark and bark and bark. Barely a comprehensible word comes from their snouts. They can't help it. Sophisticated communication is not their strong point.

"It's so loud in here," Etta says. She tries to push herself into the corner. "Remember before?" she says.

"Before?"

"Yes. Back then," she says. "When we were, you know, all together."

"Yes. Of course I do." But the truth is that I only barely remember. It's more of a feeling in my memory. Of safety. And comfort. Something we were born into but can never have back.

Another small human taps on our condo door and presses his face into the glass and yells, "Kittens!"

I nudge Etta gently. "Cover your ears," I say. Then I snuggle into Etta to block the noise. This is not exactly what I thought would happen. There's so much chatter.

"Look at this one!" someone says.

"I want that one!" another cries.

One of them tries to open our condo door.

Etta and I cuddle together. "This is exciting," I say, in an upbeat voice. I nudge her again, to remind her this is all part of the process. But I can tell that she is not so sure.

My ears prick up when I hear a *clippity-cloppity* noise approach and then my name.

"Elvis!" I hear. I poke my head out from our fluff ball. A human woman stands in front of our condo. She smiles with all her teeth and pets a long tail of hair that hangs over her shoulder.

"Carly, is it?" she calls out. "I'm Mrs. Pemberton. Can you help me over here with little Elvis?" Her voice changes when she says my name, like I'm a baby or something. "I love that name." She taps on our glass door with her fingernails as Carly approaches. "Carly, he's perfect for my daughter. She's had a hard month. Her father and I . . . well, anyway . . ."

"Oh, Mrs. Pemberton," Carly says, "your daughter will love Elvis. And he has a sister, Etta. She's precious."

I whisper to Etta, "It's happening. Our forever family, Etta. Here we go."

Carly opens our condo door and grabs me by the

scruff. The tip of my tail brushes Etta's whiskers. Carly pulls me out and tucks me under her arm, but as she reaches back to get Etta, the woman says, "Oh, no. Just one." And Carly shuts the door. *Snap-click.*

I look back at Etta. "Hey, wait a minute," I say. But Carly doesn't listen.

My heart starts pounding, and I taste something sour in my mouth.

Etta springs toward the glass and looks at me. "Elvis?" she says.

I wiggle in Carly's grasp. I try to bite her wrist, but I can barely move my head. "Etta! Etta!" I say.

Carly hands me over to the woman, whose scent is sharper than that stinky black pen.

"Are you sure you don't want them both, Mrs. Pemberton?" Carly asks.

"Yes! Yes! We are together," I say as clearly as I can.

"Just Elvis," she says. "We kind of have a full house already."

The woman, this Mrs. Pemberton, presses her face right into mine and shakes her head back and forth, and I can't breathe. "Elvis, you'll be perfect," she says in that baby talk. Her tail of hair tickles my nose.

I strain my neck in Etta's direction.

"Elvis, don't go," she says, and I feel dizzy and sick.

"Told ya," Rupert says.

The *clippity-clopping* starts up, and my view of Etta gets farther and farther away. "Etta," I call. "EEETTTA-AAAAAA!" But all I can see is the light pink of her paw pads pressed flat against the glass of our condo.

 # Chapter 3

"Carly, what about Etta?" I say.

"I know. I love you, too," she says.

I state very clearly, "Etta and I belong together!" But it's no use. Humans don't listen. They never do. If only I knew how to string the right letters together. If only I could hold that stinky black pen. I would write it out for her on the whiteboard. I would make her understand. But I can't do any of that. So, I stiffen my legs and hiss with all I've got. Before I know it, I'm being pushed into one of those cardboard carrying boxes. I press my eyes up to the peek holes and try to orient myself. I see the Second Chance Club and the posters hanging on the brick walls. Mrs. Pemberton sticks her eyes up to the peek holes and breathes hot, dry air into the carrier.

"Where are you taking me?" I say.

"Oh, Elvis," she says. "Georgina is going to love you."

"She will love Etta, too," I say.

But Mrs. Pemberton ignores me and pets her tail of hair.

Carly looks through the peek holes at me. "Goodbye, my friend. You're going to have a wonderful life. I'm so happy for you."

I jump and scratch at the cardboard. Then I run in circles, trying to find a way out. I can't see back to our condo. I can't see Etta. What is going to happen to her? Where am I going? This is all wrong.

The *clippity-clopping* starts again, and I can't keep my balance inside the carrier. I try to dig my nails into the cardboard to steady myself. It's no use. Suddenly a cool breeze hits my fur. We are in the out-of-doors. I turn around and look back at the City Shelter of Care and Comfort. The red bricks. The glass windows. One of those Old Glory's flying from the top. And then *SLAM!* I can't see a thing. I claw at the peek holes, trying to force myself through. But who am I kidding? "Etta," I say. "Etta. This wasn't supposed to happen."

Getting to wherever we are going is full of jolts and bumps. Not to mention that constant stream of noise Mrs. Pemberton makes.

She can't stop talking about Georgina. Georgina this. Georgina that. I don't care one lick about Georgina. I just want to get back to the shelter and start this whole thing over. With Etta.

Suddenly, I can see the out-of-doors again through the peek holes. We're headed to a small building. A house. With a porch and a front door. I see some grass and trees, too. It's like a cottage from Carly's fairy-tale book.

Once inside, Mrs. Pemberton sets the carrier on the floor. I look through the peek holes and try to get my bearings.

"Elvis, we're home," she says.

"No. This is not my home," I tell her.

She opens my carrier and sticks her face inside, and her tail of hair flicks my eyes. "Now, Elvis," she says, like we're good friends or something, "Georgina will be back from her father's house soon. Come on out and get used to your surroundings. This is your new home."

I look up at the woman. Her eyes blink and blink and she won't stop smiling. But that's not going to make me like her.

"Leave me alone," I say.

Naturally, she ignores me and reaches her hands into the carrier and grabs for me. I swipe at her wrist and hiss.

"Ouch!" she says. "Oh, gosh. I guess you need a moment. I'll be right back." She turns and *clippity-clops* away. Good!

I lift my head out of the cardboard box and look around. There are signs of humans everywhere. Sofas. Chairs. Tables. Rugs. I know about these things from Carly's books.

Ah! There!

A window!

That's my way out of here.

I pull myself out of the box and onto the floor and fix my eyes on my escape route. But then I hear that woman's *clippity-clops* approaching.

"Elvis!" she calls. "Are you ready to come out and see your new home?"

I quickly wedge myself behind some sort of tower. My heart is pounding so loud, I am sure she can hear it. I hold my breath.

A strange noise comes from the tower. Like a heartbeat.

Ticktock.

Ticktock.

"Elvis! Where are you?" she calls.

I can't hold my breath any longer, and just as I gasp for air, the tower erupts into an explosion of sounds.

Tingle. Tingle. Tingle.

Bong. Bong. Bong.

I dart out from behind the thing and run as fast as my legs will let me. I slide down the hall and tumble as I turn the corner into another room, searching for something, anything, to hide behind.

Mrs. Pemberton appears out of nowhere and scoops me up. "You are a little rascal," she says. She presses her face into mine and rubs her nose back and forth. Her scent blasts my nostrils, and I sneeze and cough.

If only I could wiggle out of her hands.

But she holds me out in front of her and squeezes my body. Then she walks me around pointing out all sorts of things, like I'm stupid or something. "Your litter box is over there by the back door. This is the kitchen. Here's your food bowl. Here's your water bowl." She splashes my paws in the water. Ugh! Drops flip up onto my whiskers. I shake my head back and forth and yowl, "Put me down!"

She ignores me again, so I growl and hiss.

"Aww, Elvis," she says, pressing me into the crook of

her neck and then holding me out in front of her face again. "I just want to make sure you know where everything is. I want you to be comfortable."

She can't fool me. I pull back my ears and splay my paws, showing my claws. Then I do the only thing I can think to do: I sink my teeth into her thumb!

"YOUCH!" she gasps. She loses her grip and stumbles to catch me, but I flip out of her hands and right into the water bowl. I hop over the food bowl, slip and slide on the floor, and scram out of there.

Around the corner is a set of stairs. I leap. I can barely manage these steep steps, but I strain and trip my way to the top and tear down another hallway and through an open door. I scramble across the floor, heading for some sort of cabinet or something, and tuck in quickly behind it. My heart is thumping so loudly in my ears that I can't hear anything else.

I try to calm myself, but I'm shaking, so I crouch down and hope for the best.

What do I do? How do I get out of here? What about Etta?

It's nearly impossible to think, so I concentrate on breathing.

What's that smell?

Sniff. Sniff.

I lift my nose.

Kibble.

Newspaper.

Wood shavings.

A peculiar noise rises up through my muffled ears. Shuffling. Scratching.

I strain my neck to peer out of my hiding place without fully emerging. The room is filled with all sorts of interesting things. Toys, for one. Like some of the things Carly gives us to swat around our condo. And books. Stacked neatly on a shelf. I think of Carly. Her books. Her voice. The way it rises and falls when she reads. That just reminds me of Etta, and I feel terrible all over again.

But there's that sound. *Shuffle, shuffle. Scratch, scratch.*

I step out from my hiding place and see a row of bins, like the ones that hold kibble at the shelter. Only these bins are filled with tiny, colorful bricks. Hundreds. No, thousands of shiny bricks. And so many colorful things made from these bricks. I recognize them from Carly's books: an airplane, a sailing ship, a castle, and an enormous structure in the middle of the room. It's at least two or three times as tall as me, reaching up to the ceiling. I cock my head and twitch my whiskers.

"That's the Sears Tower of Chicago," a perky voice calls out. I jump back. "Well, it's not the actual Sears Tower, of course. The real one is in Chicago, and that's a long way from San Francisco. And also, it's not called the Sears Tower anymore. Just so you know. This is a replica. Georgina and I are almost finished with it."

I peek out again, just barely.

"Come on out," the voice says. "This is the best room in the house. Do you see how the afternoon sun streams like a rainbow right through the window and lands like a pot of gold in the middle of the floor?"

I look at the floor. Rainbow? Pot of gold? Please.

But that voice. Where is it coming from?

I scan the room again. I should have seen it earlier. In the corner. Another structure. A home of some sort. Like a plastic palace. With tunnels. Platforms. Walkways. Connecting this to that and here to there. It has food bowls and waterspouts and fluff.

Fluff on the floor.

Fluff in the tunnels.

Fluff pushing out through the roof.

So much fluff.

If only Etta were here. We had seen something like this at the shelter. The creature inside was fascinating. It sent us both into a tizzy.

Sure enough, on a platform at the very top of the palace, is a hamster.

"Mo Pemberton, at your service," the little guy says. Then he pops the door in the ceiling of his home and scrambles out and down to the floor.

A tickle wiggles around in my stomach. I snap my tail. And twitch my whiskers.

I creep forward into the middle of the room and breathe in a lungful of the little guy. He smells . . . I can't describe it. Tasty!

I simply can't help myself—

I spring forward and pounce!

Sunday, July 4, 5:27 PM

Georgina. You OK?

Daddy was supposed to drop you off at 5 PM.

I just tried to call you. Please call or text.

Be there soon.

Oh, thank goodness.

Do you have a pic on ur phone from Chicago?

A picture?

In front of the Sears Tower. With Daddy.

I don't know.

Hurry home. I have a surprise. 😊

Chapter 4

"Holy habitat!" the hamster cries out and dives behind his plastic palace. "Now hold on just a minute!"

My aggression is kind of a surprise to me. I pull back and sit still.

"You are energetic," he says. "And what style! Why, you've got more colors than a Lucky Charms cereal box. I know because I just dismantled one yesterday."

"These are my calico colors," I say, lifting my chin.

"Marvelous," he says.

The furry fellow tiptoes out from behind his plastic palace and inches his way over to me.

"You got a name?" he says. He has graying fur on his ears and a paunchy stomach. His hands are delicate, with long fingers that he holds together and taps at their tips, like he's thinking or planning.

"Elvis," I say, snapping my tail for effect.

"Well, you must be our new roommate. We heard we were getting a new one."

"No, no," I say. "I'm not staying here." I press my face a little closer to Mo's and take in another big whiff. My stomach growls.

"Ah," Mo says. He grabs hold of one of his long whiskers and holds it between his thumb and forefinger.

"This is all a big mistake," I say. "I was supposed to stay with my sister. We were supposed to be together."

I watch Mo the hamster begin to twist that poor little whisker round and round. He twists while he speaks. "I see," he says. "Well, you must be tired from your travels. Georgina and I are almost finished with the Sears Tower. Let me tell you about it. It's quite remarkable."

"I'm not interested in your tower," I say. This is the most ridiculous thing I've ever heard. A hamster who wants to talk about a tower. Please. "I need to get back to Etta. She's my sister. She needs me."

"Yes," he says. "Of course." He stops twisting and scurries over to the Sears Tower and climbs up to the top and waves. "You need to know, first and foremost," he calls out, "that the Sears Tower is made from bundled tubes. See how they have the appearance of steps?"

"No," I say. This guy is nuts. I look around and spot a window. An escape route! How to get to it?

While I'm thinking, Mr. Mo keeps right on talking.

"Tubes of varying heights are bundled together, forming a collection of towers . . ." *blah blah blah*, "resist outside forces," *blah blah blah*, ". . . wind and gravity . . ." *blah blah blah*. "What do you think of that?"

"Whatever," I say, zeroing in on a chair. I jump up onto it and try to angle myself closer to the window. "I don't have time for this, sir."

"Everyone has time for architecture," he says. Then he lifts his tiny hamster head and yells, "LAVERNE! OUR NEW ROOMMATE WANTS TO LEARN ABOUT THE SEARS TOWER!"

"No, I don't," I say. "Arcs and textures? Please."

"Architecture," he says. "Building design. I'm a builder, you see. What do you do?"

"I'm a kitten," I say. "I do what kittens do. Duh."

"Oh, I see. You haven't figured out your raison d'être."

"My raisin what?" Now I'm getting frustrated.

"Your purpose," he says. "Everyone has one. Laverne—up there on the bureau—she's our guard fish." Mo nods at the tall piece of furniture under the window.

Sure enough, I look up, and a pair of goggly eyes stares down at me through a glass bowl.

"Laverne keeps us posted on the comings and goings around here. From her position, she can see all the way down the hall. She is always on the lookout. She gave me a warning when you arrived."

I realize that I may be able to jump up there from the chair, so I dig my nails into the fabric and spring off. My landing is shaky, and I slide and almost knock right into the glass bowl. I get a close-up view. Fascinating!

Apparently, there is more to a fish than just eyes. Laverne is solid orange. Her fur is feathery, and her black, glassy eyes protrude from her face on either side of her head. She glides easily through the water in continuous circles. There's a rock in there, with a hole in it. Like a hiding place. I've never seen anything like this in my life. Bubbles float. Tiny waves roll. The floor is covered with sparkly blue pebbles, and there is a glittery box in the center with letters on it. I see a *T*. I know *T* from the alphabet book, but I can't remember what it stands for, so I don't know what it says. Laverne jolts in and out of her rock and around and around.

The whole thing is tremendously thrilling, and I feel another tickle in my tummy. I reach into the bowl and touch the water.

Laverne jumps out with a flip and yells, "KEEP OUT!" Then that crazy orange fish nips at my toes.

I back up and turn my attention to the window, which I realize is right next to me. I try to push it open, but it doesn't budge. I see the out-of-doors. Trees, cars, other houses. And believe it or not, another one of those Old Glories, flapping in the breeze just outside this window.

Suddenly, that crazy orange fish splashes and yells some more. "INCOMING! THE KID!"

I jump at the volume of her gurgling voice and almost fall to the floor.

In the doorway is a human girl with skinny arms held tightly at her side.

I try to hide behind Laverne's bowl but realize you can see right through it. So I jump to the chair and onto the floor and scramble for the bookshelf. Behind the books, I watch as the girl leans down and hands Mo a cardboard something or other. Mo holds it up in the air and jumps twice. "Thanks, Georgina," he says.

Aha! Georgina.

Georgina approaches the bookshelf, and I brace for a confrontation. Surely this human will try to pick me up. She'll probably poke and prod at my body, pull my tail, and squeeze me so I can't breathe. She might even go get that annoying Mrs. Pemberton.

I close my eyes and hold my breath.

But nothing happens.

When I finally open my eyes, the girl is sitting on the floor in front of me.

She lifts her brows. Her brown eyes are wide and soft around the edges. Her hair is parted on the side and held in place with a shiny pink something or other. On her shirt is a picture of a big, red apple. And a whole bunch of buildings. Towers, like Mo was talking about.

She slowly reaches her hand out toward me, but I pull back and crouch. She sets her hand on the floor and taps her fingers lightly. "Hello," she whispers.

I lean forward, down on my belly, and inch toward those dancing fingers. They are delicate and strong-looking at the same time. They look like fun. But I'm not going to fall for any human tricks, that's for sure. Not after everything that's happened today.

Her fingers stop moving. She looks right into my eyes and blinks three times. I think about blinking back but change my mind. Then she reaches into one of the bins and pulls out a yellow brick and pushes it toward me. It's shiny and tempting. But I stay low and wait. It is nearly impossible. I don't move a whisker for what seems like hours.

Georgina watches me. She doesn't try to poke me or pull my tail. She doesn't push her face into mine, and she speaks very softly. "Welcome," she says. Surely she's trying to fool me.

I decide to take a chance and come out from my hiding spot—but only a little bit. I make sure to stay away from Georgina, but I keep my eyes on her, just in case.

Georgina opens a very large book and flips through the pages.

"That's our architecture book," Mo says, skittering over and tapping on it like he rules the world. "Georgina got it for her birthday. It's our inspiration!" He rambles on some more about the Sears Tower like some kind of know-it-all. He talks about the architect who designed it—Bruce somebody or other—and the year it was completed—nineteen seventy-something. And then Laverne calls out again, and I almost fall over dead.

"INCOMING! MOMMY!"

Apparently, "Mommy" is the same thing as Mrs. Pemberton, because there she is, front and center. "Georgina! Oh, good. Elvis is out of hiding. I am so glad. Isn't he the cutest?" Mrs. Pemberton snaps me up before I can get away. "I know things have been difficult, Georgina," Mrs. Pemberton says. "And I thought a new, precious pet would be comforting. Elvis is all yours, Georgina."

"What? No, I'm not!" I say.

Mrs. Pemberton holds me in front of Georgina, who gently takes me into her arms and sets me back down on the floor. I scramble back behind the bookshelf.

"He's adorable, Mommy. But a new kitten needs a quiet space."

"Yes, of course he does. You're right," Mrs. Pemberton says, backing off and putting her hands on her hips.

Ha! Georgina showed her. Even still, Mommy Pemberton keeps right on talking. "We have the Fourth of July block party in a little while. You and I are going together, Georgina. It's going to be fun. And there will be other kids. For you to play with." She grabs her tail of hair and tilts her head. "What do you say?"

"I don't want to play with other kids," Georgina says.

"Oh, Georgina," Mommy Pemberton says. She smiles and wiggles around. "There's going to be sparklers. And cupcakes."

"Fine," Georgina says. "I'll go."

Georgina picks up the little yellow brick and gets another one from the bin. She presses the two together. *SNAP!* Then she turns the joined pieces over and over in her fingers.

"Mo and I are just about finished with the Sears Tower," she says.

"I see that, Georgina. It's quite impressive."

"Did you look for that picture on your phone, Mommy? From Chicago?"

"That was a terrible trip, Georgina," Mrs. Mommy says, shaking her head. "Honey, I'm glad you're working with your LEGOs. It's a worthwhile STEM activity, and I support it. But wouldn't you like me to schedule a playdate for you one of these days?"

"I don't need a playdate. I have skyscrapers to build. Will you look on your phone?"

"Of course. I'll look for it," Mommy says, petting her tail. "I have a few emails to answer right now, so grab your sweatshirt and meet me downstairs in ten minutes."

Mommy stands there and sighs. Georgina looks up and nods. Then Mommy turns and leaves.

Humans are terrible at conversating. It's embarrassing to watch. Just like the dogs at the shelter. Bark, bark, bark. Maybe one intelligent word, if you're lucky.

Mo scampers into one of the bins and comes out with a shiny, black brick. He hands it to Georgina, who adds it to the Sears Tower with a *SNAP!* I like the sound. Georgina adds another one. *SNAP! CLICK!* It reminds me of the shelter.

The two continue with this for a few minutes, then Georgina pats Mo's head with her finger. She looks over at me, says my name, "Elvis," and leaves the room. That's my cue.

"It was nice meeting you," I say to Mo, who seems to be counting bricks. "But I have to leave, too."

"Are you sure?" he says, twisting that poor little whisker again. "We could use your help around here. You heard Georgina. We've got skyscrapers to build. And summer vacation doesn't last forever."

I shake my head. Skyscrapers. Please. And, whatever summer vacation is, it has nothing to do with me and Etta. So I head for the door. I look out into the hallway and then back at Georgina's room.

"I hope you reconsider," Mo calls out. "Either way, steer clear of Clementine."

Clementine? Whatever.

I wave Mo off and step over the threshold and into the darkening hallway.

 Chapter 5

The hallway is long and wide. I'm not sure where to go from here. I see another window down the way, so I head in that direction.

The window is so high up that I'm not sure how I'm going to reach it. Jumping is really my only option. I crouch and push off my hind legs with all I've got and grab onto the edge. But I slip off backward and do a flip in midair. I surprise myself and land on all fours. Wow!

I shake off the shock, suck in a lungful of air, leap, and fall again.

There's got to be something to step on. But there is nothing in the hallway except for a large board on the wall. It reminds me of the white board at the shelter, only this one is the color of kibble: brown. Pinned to it is something I easily recognize: a calendar. Strangely, this calendar does not have a single *X* on it. It's got other letters, though, that I know from Carly's alphabet book. *D*s and *M*s. In every box. Everyone knows that you're supposed to put *X*es in each box, to mark the day. This calendar is all wrong. Oh, it doesn't matter anyway. I've got to get to that window.

I peer around looking for ideas but can't come up with anything, so I decide to abandon this plan and head for the stairs. Just then, a light flashes in the window followed by *POP! CRACKLE! BANG!*

I jump straight up and scramble, but the floor is slippery. I roll head-over-tail to get away from another enormous blast. *ZIP! ZIP! BANG!* I scramble through the first door I see and slide underneath the bed inside. That ticking tower downstairs must have finally exploded.

The popping and zapping continues all around me, and I'm sure something is going to crash down and ruin everything forever. The room shakes, windows rattle, and flashing lights bounce off the walls. I squint and feel dizzy, and my ears pound and ache, and there's no way these bed skirts can protect me. I squeeze my eyes shut and brace for destruction.

Maybe I should run back into Georgina's room, but I can barely breathe. My tail twitches, my whiskers

tremble, and the fur on my back stands straight up. I don't know what to do.

Finally, there is a break in the commotion, and my heartbeat slows. An echo rings in my ears, but I am able to take a deep breath.

I open my eyes to see the silhouette of another feline sitting right in front of me. I see the sparkle of a glittery collar.

"What are you doing under here?" the feline says.

"Part of the world blew up," I say.

"Perfectly pitiful. That's just the fireworks, you fluffy imp."

"Oh, right. The fireworks," I say. "Of course."

"Fireworks are the celebratory flamboyance of the entertainment-centric human race. They cannot be avoided on Independence Day."

I don't know what the heck this feline is talking about, but I play along. "I know," I say. "It was quite loud. The whole place almost came crashing down—ha!"

"Well, the world is a loud place, and things come crashing down all the time, so you'd better get used to it. I take it you're the consolation prize." This feline has a way with words, and most of them I've never heard before.

"Maybe I am," I say with my chin up.

I watch the cat move from beneath the bed and into the light of the room. She's pasty yellow with a splattering of brown along her back and a single splotch of orange on her hip. Long, tufted fur frames her face. And her tail is bent and twisted. What a mess.

Then it occurs to me. "Are you Clementine?"

"What's it to you?" she says.

"I thought you were supposed to be scary," I say.

"BOO!" she says, and throws her head back laughing. I lean backward. Please.

"That ratty mouse and his fishy friend are telling stories again, aren't they," she says, preening her orange patch.

"Mo is a hamster," I say.

"Hamster, mouse, rat, guinea pig. It's all the same to me. Rodents! They're ruinous."

"Well, my name is Elvis, and I was just on my way out."

"I know exactly who you are. Mommy had to find something for Georgina to make up for all the changes around here. And you're that something."

"Of course," I say, like I've known it all along. But then curiosity gets me. "What changes?"

"I'm talking about Mommy and Daddy. Daddy doesn't live here anymore, in case you hadn't noticed." She licks her paw and smooths the uneven fur on her face.

"Sure, I noticed," I say—a bit of a lie. "But it's no concern of mine since I'm about to leave."

"Good," she says. "Because it's pure chaos in this house, and we don't need any other characters to add to the drama. And, by the way, this is Mommy's room, and it's off-limits!"

She glares at me and begins to slink away. And that's when I realize it. I've seen her before. On one of the posters at the shelter. She's practically famous!

"You're from the Second Chance Club," I say.

Clementine stops in her tracks. She turns back around and snarls, "How do you know about the Second Chance Club?"

"It's at the City Shelter of Care and Comfort," I say. "Everyone deserves a second chance. It's common knowledge. Not that most ever get one, from what I've . . . heard."

"You don't know anything," she hisses like Rupert. "Now get out of my chamber! And keep your pitiful paws off Mommy. She's mine. We don't want anything to do with you or that ridiculous rodent."

"Alright! That's enough, Clementine." It's Mo. He's suddenly standing in the doorway. "There's no need to be rude to Elvis. For goodness sake, it's his first day here."

"Oh, what do you care?" Clementine says, flicking her crooked tail. "P.S. Mo, I'm feeling a little snack attack coming on."

"Wait! Don't fight over me," I say. "This might be my first day here, but it's also my last. Remember? I'm leaving."

"Come on, Elvis," Mo says. "Let's give Clementine her space."

I don't know why, but I follow Mo out the door. I turn back and look at Clementine. She sits and grooms the orange spot on her hip. She sees me and curls her tail around her body, sort of. I feel sorry for her tail.

Back in Georgina's room, I need to know. "What's her deal?" I ask.

"She's got a history," Mo says.

"What kind of history? Why was she in the Second Chance Club?"

"Whatever the reason, it has affected her outlook on life. The way she sees the world."

"Oh, yes. Of course," I say.

"You've got to keep your eyes focused on the positive. Don't look back," Mo says.

"I agree," I say. "Focus on the positive." I hold my head up, not letting Mo know that I can't think of anything positive at all right now. It seems I am stuck in this house. I can't figure out how to get out and back to the shelter. And even if I could, it's dark out there, and I won't be able to orient myself. And on top of all of that, I'm exhausted.

Mo scurries right up to my face and puts his hands on my cheeks. I'm so tired that I ignore the urge in my stomach. "Elvis, sometimes finding the positive takes concentration," he says.

"I know that," I say. And then I think about concentrating on the positive and nothing happens.

I stretch my neck around a bit and watch Mo. He skitters across the floor, climbs back up to the top of his plastic palace, pops the door open, and crawls inside. Something about that is all wrong!

"Hey," I say. "How come you're not locked up in that plastic house of yours?"

"Elvis, this is a home, not a prison," he says.

"But why on earth would you stay here if you could leave?" I ask.

"Simple. I like it here."

"Well, I don't like it here, and I'm leaving," I say.

"I know. You already said that. But we're starting on the Transamerica Pyramid soon. It's the skyscraper near Daddy's office, and you're not going to want to miss that," Mo says. "In the meantime, I need to get some shut-eye. Good night, Elvis." He crawls into one of his fluff-filled tunnels and disappears.

The Trans-a-whatever it is. Please.

There is no denying that I'm too tired to try to leave tonight. I crawl under Georgina's bed. It's like the bed from that one princess fairy tale of Carly's with lots of pillows and blankets. Etta would love it. I find a pile of wrinkled clothes under here, so I start treading. I'll leave in the morning when the sun is up and I have more energy.

I close my eyes and try to get comfortable. It's not easy. Every so often the room lights up and the windows rattle. The "celebratory flamboyance," I think, covering my ears. Why does it have to be so loud?

I'm still awake when Georgina climbs into bed above me. She tosses around for a few minutes. The bed creaks and squeaks. I hear a few splashy *plips* coming from Laverne's bowl, too. And then, finally, after a long sigh, I hear Georgina's slow, soft breath. It rumbles gently. Just like Etta's. But Georgina is not Etta!

Oh, Etta. Are you in our condo at the shelter? Are you curled in the corner, treading alone on the hard, cold glass? Who will be there to greet you in the morning and gently nudge you awake? Who will tumble with you after breakfast? Who will be there to answer all your questions? It should be me, and it is not. I am here. You are—I don't know where you are, and I can't stand it.

Monday, July 5, 8:27 AM

Daddy, look what we got!

Wow, G!

Who is this?

Elvis! Mommy got him.

Holy moly! Lucky you!

I know. 🖤🖤💕

 # Chapter 6

I wake to the sound of whooshing and rattling.

I stretch my arms and legs and yawn so loudly that a fierce growl escapes my mouth. I poke my head out from under the bed and creep forward, and for a moment, I can't remember where I am.

"Good morning," Mo says from inside his plastic palace. He's on his wheel, running. "It's good to get your exercise out of the way first thing, I always say."

This guy's joy is annoying, and I need to get the heck out of here. If only my stomach wasn't screaming.

"What do you have on the docket for today?" Mo asks.

"The docket?" Here we go with more code words.

"The agenda. The schedule," he says.

My heart says that I am headed out immediately, back to the shelter to find Etta. But going to sleep last night without a snack really did me in. "Breakfast," I say.

"Marvelous! A good meal in the morning makes all the difference," Mo says.

"Whatever," I say, and slip out the door. I'm in that long hallway again, and I can see the window and the door that leads to Mommy's room. I find the stairs and hop down swiftly.

In the kitchen, Mrs. Mommy *clippity-clops* around and sips loudly on her human drink, while Georgina sits at the counter. Clementine is at the food bowl. I don't even consider butting in.

"Georgina," Mommy says. "You have a busy day today. I'm dropping you off at the library for Reading Circle. My workday is crammed, so Jasmine will pick you up from the library and be your chauffeur. You've got swimming lessons and piano. And did you check the calendar? *M*s all week until Friday. Then it's a *D* day again. Daddy says he might take you to San Francisco this weekend."

"You said we were going to New York City this summer," Georgina says. "ALL THREE OF US TOGETHER."

"Georgina, I don't know if we're going to be able to do that," Mommy says.

"But we talked about it with Daddy."

"I know we did, sweetie. But sometimes plans change."

"But you said—"

"Georgina." Mommy sits down next to Georgina and takes her hand. "We're all doing the best we can."

Georgina looks down at me, but she doesn't smile. Mommy just sits there. I'm glad that neither one of them feels the need to grab me and squeeze me to death. What a relief!

At least now I know what the *D* on the calendar stands for. Of course I know.

Technically, I have a daddy, too, not that I've ever met him. And a mother. I'm sure of it. I think of *before*, back then. I feel it, anyway. The comfort. The safety. And Etta. Hey, if the *D* stands for Daddy, then the *M* must stand for—

"Elvis!" Mommy suddenly scoops me up. She puts her face up to mine and then takes a huge whiff of my tummy. My tummy! Please. "We just love you so much," she says in that baby voice. "Kittens are such a joy. Isn't that right, Georgina? And, I bet Clementine is happy to have a feline friend."

I try to look at Georgina, but I can't move my head. My shoulders are scrunched up to the tips of my ears, and I'm completely helpless.

Mommy holds me out to Georgina. Georgina gently takes me into her arms. She kisses my head and says my name, "Elvis." Then she sets me on the floor. I skedaddle behind the counter and try to hide. I certainly don't need to be kissed on the head like that.

Clementine saunters past me toward the hallway. "Out of my way," she scowls.

I scoot up to the food bowl with high hopes. Empty! Not a crumb in there. My stomach churns and I lick at the edge of the bowl, hoping for something.

"Georgina, shuffle on upstairs and put a comb through that hair, will you," Mommy says. "And grab your sweatshirt. I need to answer an email, then we're out of here in ten."

Georgina refills the food and water bowls and crouches down near me. I pull back into the corner, suspicious. But she just smiles at me and leaves. Good. At last I can fill my tummy.

After I eat and wash down the kibble with a few laps of water, I head down the hall to the front door. I spot that window again, the one by the sofa, and consider checking it out.

"What are you still doing here, anyway?" Clementine says from around the corner.

"I'm leaving, okay?" I say. "It's not that easy."

"It's about the easiest thing there is, you fluffy imp," she says.

Clementine comes into view and sits squarely in front of me. She leans over and grooms the orange patch on her hip.

"Hide behind Big Ben." She nods at that ticking tower then dramatically continues licking.

"Wait for Mommy to get the tote bag." Lick, lick.

"The book bag." Lick.

"And all the other bags that define the human existence." Lick. Lick.

"She can't bring everything outside to that motor car of hers all at once." Lick.

"You mean the rambling contraption?" I say.

"It's called a car, Elvis."

"Yes. A car. I know," I say.

"Anyway, she always leaves this door, right here, wide open." Lick. Lick.

"All you have to do is wait." Lick. Lick. Lick.

"It's easy as *A, B, C*."

"*A, B, C*? Do you know the alphabet?" I say, shocked.

"Oh, for the love of furballs! JUST LEAVE WHEN THE DOOR IS OPEN! Sheesh!"

"Okay, I know," I say. "I'm not stupid."

"Your absence will be better for all of us." Lick. Lick.

Clementine hops up onto one of the chairs in the big room near the front door and nestles into a blanket draped over the back.

I'm suspicious of the whole thing. But at this point, I've got nothing to lose. So I sit behind Big Ben, the exploding tower—and wait. And why is it called Big Ben, anyway?

 # Chapter 7

In a matter of minutes, Mommy marches down the hallway and starts doing exactly what Clementine said she would. I glance at Clementine on the back of the big chair. She smirks at me and preens her paws like a glamour puss.

Mommy brings over a big bag, filled to the brim with who knows what, and sets it by the front door. Then she brings over another bag, filled with books. I watch her shuffle into the kitchen for yet another item, which is not a bag, but more like a box or something. Finally, she places a sweater on top of all of it. I remain undetected behind Big Ben.

"Georgina! Hop to!" Mommy yells. "Time to go!" She stands and pets her tail of hair. She looks around and spots Clementine on the back of the chair. Clementine immediately jumps off and circles Mommy's feet, yowling and begging for attention. Mommy leans down and pats the top of her head and says, "Aren't you so happy to have a new kitty friend?"

Clementine looks over at me and very clearly says, "No!" But Mommy doesn't hear her. She just opens the door and carries two of the bags outside. I can see past the porch to the front lawn, the sidewalk, and even across the street. A shiver runs from the back of my neck to the tip of my tail. It's my chance.

I perk up my ears. Noises from the out-of-doors come in loud and clear. Birds chirp. Cars motor by. A horn honks.

All sorts of scents waft under my nose. Sweet. Fresh. Inviting.

The cool air ruffles my fur. I breathe in a lungful.

"It's now or never, kid," Clementine says.

She's right. I push off my back legs and spring through the door.

I duck behind a flowerpot on the porch and contemplate which direction to take. Where is the shelter from here? I realize I have no idea what to do next. I'm in the out-of-doors, and it's so big.

Mommy stands half-in, half-out of her car. I glance over my shoulder to the house. A jolt of energy pushes through my body and I leap down the porch steps and land in the grass. Cold. Squishy. Spongy.

I skitter across the lawn as fast as I can and hop onto the sidewalk. To one side, a man walks a dog in my direction. To the other, a gaggle of kids skip and shout as they approach. My heart pounds in my chest.

I step off the sidewalk into the gutter and onto the dark pavement of the street. I'm sure I'll know what to do if I can just get across the street. But it's hot on my paws. I do a one-paw-at-a-time dance to keep from burning my pads. Water pools in the gutter on the other side. It's the relief I need. I make a run for it.

"Elvisssssss!" I hear.

I turn around mid-crossing and see Georgina charging through the front yard.

A car honks. And skids. Something shiny blinds me.

I trip. And stumble. And roll across the blacktop, head over tail. Blue sky and black pavement. Blue sky. Black pavement. Blue. Black. Blue.

Then Georgina's voice again, "Noooo!"

I try to find my footing. When I look up, I am suddenly lifted and squeezed into human arms.

Georgina tumbles with me, splashing into the gutter.

Muddy water fills my mouth. My ears throb, and my foreleg aches. I spit out the nasty water and catch the scent of blood.

I look at Georgina and mew. Short, quick sounds that I can't control. This wasn't supposed to happen. It's all wrong. Again.

"It's okay, Elvis," Georgina says. "I've got you." She looks in my eyes and speaks. Her voice is smooth and silky. "Everything is going to be just fine," she says. "I promise." She cuddles me and holds me and snuggles me. She's so soft. And warm.

Mommy comes running across the street screaming. "Georgina! Oh my gosh! Are you alright? What happened?"

"He didn't get hit, Mommy," Georgina says. "We tumbled out of the way."

"Oh, thank goodness."

Georgina stands and keeps me close to her chest. A frantic human talks to Mommy. I hear things like "I'm sorry" and "didn't see" and "what a relief." For the first time since I arrived, I am happy to be held.

Then we are back in the house, and Mommy is cleaning Georgina's skinned knees and bloody elbows.

I peer out from under Georgina's arms.

Clementine appears and stares up at me. "Congratulations," she says.

"What?" I say, blinking and confused.

Clementine leans over and licks at the orange patch on her hip. "You're a true escape artist. Minus the actual escape, of course."

 # Chapter 8

Georgina sets me gently on the floor and I immediately get up to walk. A pain shoots through my paw, all the way up my leg, so I sit down swiftly and hold my foreleg off the ground. I'm afraid to step on my paw.

"Ha! Maybe *you* belong in the Second Chance Club," Clementine says.

"It's not so bad," I say.

"Mommy, Elvis is injured. Look!" Georgina says.

"I see that," Mommy replies. "Something is wrong with his foot."

"We need to take him to the vet," Georgina says.

"Yes. I suppose we do. This whole day is down the drain. I'd better cancel with Jasmine. And I shouldn't have gotten another cat. I don't know what I was thinking." Mommy furrows her brow and pets her tail of hair. "Georgina, let's get his carrier."

Georgina whispers to me as she puts me in that awful cardboard box. "The vet will get you all fixed up, Elvis. Don't worry about a thing."

Not the vet! Everyone grabbing at me. The prodding! The needles! That terrible thing they use to take your temperature. The fur on my back stands straight up. The vet at the shelter was so nosy. Hey! The vet at the shelter. We're going back to the shelter!

In the car, Georgina sticks her fingers through the peek holes of the carrier, and I lick and nip at them excitedly. Who ever thought I'd be excited to go to the vet? Everything suddenly feels better. They're taking me back to Etta!

On the way there, we bump and jolt like before. It might be called a car, but it's still a rambling contraption that knocks me around my carrier. But when it stops and quiets down, I don't see the red brick building. Or the huge glass windows. And there's no Old Glory flying at the top. I've never seen this building before. Now my leg hurts even more.

Inside, the vet hops around me, checking every single strand of fur. Georgina is there stroking my back. But then the vet takes me into another room by myself. I ready my claws, but the ones on my injured paw won't activate, so I yowl and hiss.

The vet places me on a table and fiddles with my paw, moving it in all directions. She attaches something cold to my leg and wraps it tight with pink sticky stuff. Then she gives me a shot. At this point, I've had enough. I don't bother with any pleasantries, I just bite.

"I know you're scared, sweetie," she says.

"No, I'm not scared," I say. Because I'm not. I'm just frustrated. And angry. And sad. And now I have this pink thing on my leg, and I can barely move it.

After what seems like forever, she finally takes me back to Georgina and Mommy.

"It's fractured," she says. "Elvis is wearing a splint. You're going to need to keep it dry. But most importantly, you've got to restrict his activity for six weeks."

"Oh no," Georgina says.

"He'll be okay, Georgina," Mommy says. "Don't worry."

The vet pats my head. "We've given him something for the pain, too. So he'll probably take a nice long nap today."

Just as she says this, the room moves in circles around me. I close my eyes, but my head feels so heavy.

How will I ever get back to the shelter now? "Etta," I say. "I have to get to Etta."

"Oh, Elvis. You're such a sweet thing," the vet says. But she's ruined everything. All I want to do is knock her upside the head. Too bad I can't even lift my own head.

Georgina pulls me into her arms and sets me in the carrier. I look at her through the peek holes. Her eyes sparkle. I can barely keep my own eyes open. But those eyes. Then a familiar noise surrounds me. A soft rumble. "Oh, Etta," I say again. Am I hearing things? Etta, is that you?

I suddenly realize in my fuzzy, dizzy state, that the soft, comforting rumble is coming from my own broken body.

Daddy!

Elvis got injured.

Oh, no! What happened?

He got outside and almost got hit by a car.

Yikes!

Broken leg?

Yes. 😞

He's in good hands with you, G.

Is this the pic you wanted?

Yes.

Thank you, Daddy. ♥

 # Chapter 9

When I open my eyes, I am curled up in the pile of clothes underneath Georgina's bed.

Mo is standing right in front of me. "Holy habitat!" he says. "Can you see me?"

"Yes, I can see you," I say. Please.

"What happened to you?"

"I was just crossing the street."

"Streets are terrible, Elvis. Terrible!"

"I know," I say. "I think Georgina saved me."

"Georgina is a gem," Mo says.

"I broke my leg. I have a splint," I say.

"I see that." Mo crawls up onto the pink thing and knocks on it. "It's as hard as a rock," he says. "Very interesting. What type of material is it?"

I lift my head. The room turns in circles. "How would I know?" I say.

"I'm sorry about your accident," Mo says. "But the good news is that you're safe. And you're here. We're getting ready to build the Transamerica Pyramid. If you think about it, Elvis. This is all perfect timing."

It doesn't seem like perfect timing to me. It seems like terrible timing. What will Etta do without me? I'm letting her down. She is alone. Isn't it my responsibility to get back to her? Isn't that what a good brother would do?

I try to stand. But it's no use. My leg hurts and my head wobbles. Looking out from under the bed, I see Georgina sitting on the floor sorting bricks. The Sears Tower has been moved up high onto the shelf, where all of Georgina's structures are. In front of it is a picture. It's Georgina and Mommy and a human man. They look cold.

The pink stuff on my leg feels tight. I bite at it and pull the sticky stuff, but I can't get to my fur. And I've got an itch. There is no other way to say it: I am stuck.

"I guess I'll be here a while," I say to Mo.

"Good," he replies. Then he scurries away and heads over to Georgina. He presents a single white brick to her like it is some sort of precious gift. Please.

 # Chapter 10

Over the next few days, I hardly do anything but stay under the bed and watch Georgina and Mo build the Transamerica Pyramid. I'm still not quite sure what the Transamerica Pyramid is, but I like watching how easily Georgina and Mo work together, like they know exactly what to do each step of the way.

Mo hands bricks to Georgina.

Georgina snaps them into place.

Every now and then, Mo skitters back and looks at their progress. Is he nodding to Georgina? Is she nodding back?

The only sound the two make is the *snap-snap-snap* of the bricks. They don't even talk to each other. But considering that humans don't listen, what would be the point?

The sound of the tiny white bricks connecting is pleasing. I enjoy watching how they fit together just

right. After a while, the whole thing starts to look like something. It gets taller and taller, and after a couple of days, Mo crawls up to the very tip top and says, "Done!"

Georgina looks over at me. Her eyes sparkle, and I can tell she is happy about the Transamerica Pyramid.

She takes a deep breath and looks at their creation and then back at me. She reaches under the bed and strokes my back. "I'm going to San Francisco with Daddy this weekend," she says. "We were supposed to go on a family vacation to New York City, but now I don't think we're going."

I press my head into the palm of her hand.

"This is the schedule," she says. "Mommy says it is our new normal and that we'll all adjust to it soon." She slumps her shoulders. "But Mommy is wrong."

I love Georgina's voice, and I wish she would keep talking. It eases the pain in my leg. She picks me up and places me on a pillow next to the Transamerica Pyramid. It's such a strange structure. All white and tall and pointy at the top. Then she scratches me under the chin and says says, "I'll be back after the weekend, Elvis."

Georgina says goodbye to Mo and Laverne, too, and I slip off the pillow and crawl back under the bed.

Mo follows me, chattering on about this skyscraper.

"The base of the Transamerica Pyramid takes up an entire city block." *Blah blah blah.* Mo twists his whisker. "And the foundation was made with 1,750 truckloads of concrete!" *Blah blah blah.* "Isn't that marvelous?"

"Marvelous," I say. "Is everything marvelous, Mo?"

"Yes, it is," he says, not knowing I was just kidding. He can't stop talking. At this point, I am forced to listen. "Did you know that the Transamerica Pyramid was designed to survive earthquakes? It survived the Loma Prieta earthquake of 1989. It never fell over, Elvis. Highways, houses, roads, even a bridge, fell down in that earthquake. But the Transamerica Pyramid just swayed from side to side, like it was meant to do. It was undamaged!" Mo is so excited talking about it that he races back and forth in front of me. He does a standing flip. "It's a modern-day miracle!" he shouts.

I think about getting up and finding a new spot to curl into—maybe downstairs. But the pink splint makes my foot so heavy. Even just picking it up and taking one step is a big effort. Clementine is right. I belong in the Second Chance Club. I decide my best bet is to stay put for now and just endure Mo's architecture lecture. Architecture lecture. Ha!

"How do you know all this?" I finally ask.

Mo scampers over to the bookshelf and points to Georgina's architecture book. "*The Big Book of American Architecture*," he says.

"Can you read or something?" I ask. "Because I know the alphabet."

"I recognize a few letters, sure," he says. "But there's something else I'm really good at."

"Twisting your whiskers?" I say.

"Ha-ha. You're funny." He lets go of a whisker he'd just grabbed. "I listen. A fellow can learn an awful lot by listening. Georgina loves to read. She read half this book to me before you even got here."

"I know all about reading. Listening that is," I say. "From Carly. She used to read to Etta and me. At the shelter. That's how I know the alphabet."

"That's excellent, Elvis," Mo says.

I don't tell Mo that I wish I knew what all the letters stood for and how to arrange them in rows that make sense.

"It's a world of wonder, Elvis," Mo says. "And we're lucky enough to get to live in it."

I honestly don't know how one small rodent can be so happy about every single thing on earth. "Don't you know I might never see my sister again!" I say.

My leg throbs, and my heart hurts, too.

Mo skitters over to me. Right up to my face, like he does, and puts his hands on my cheeks. He opens his mouth to speak and—

"INCOMING! DANGER!"

We both snap our attention to Clementine, who sa-shays into the room.

She circles the Transamerica Pyramid. "How's the fractured feline today?" she hisses.

"Feeling great," I say—not completely true.

"Good. Then you can hit the road for real," she says. She reaches her forelegs up the side of the pyramid and stretches.

"Hey, be careful, Clementine. Georgina and Mo just finished it. Don't ruin it," I say.

"Mo. Ha! As if," she says. Then she leans into the side of the thing and flicks her crooked tail at the base and gives it a head butt.

Mo scrambles over to her and stands on his hind legs. "Please, Clementine. Don't do anything destructive."

"Destructive?" she says. "I thought your pointy little pyramid could withstand the largest of earthquakes. I'm just a diminutive, fragile feline." She leans harder into the bricks and the pyramid tips.

I pop out from under the bed, ignoring the blast of pain in my leg and position myself on the other side of the pyramid to try and keep it from tipping further. It leans onto my back, and I am worried I can't hold it.

Mo jumps up and down, pleading. "This structure is so important to Georgina. Don't you know that, Clementine? I am begging you to leave it be."

Clementine doesn't care. She leaps to the top and brings the whole thing crashing down. Chunks of the sides break off and little white bricks fly everywhere. I duck as pieces land all around me. Mo runs for cover, and Clementine shakes herself free of the rubble. "A modern-day miracle?" she says. "Ha! There's no such thing."

I can't believe she's done this. Suddenly, my leg throbs worse than before. Clementine just licks at her orange patch and turns and walks out the door.

"This is terrible. Just terrible," Mo says.

"Georgina's Transamerica Pyramid," is all I can say.

Even Laverne splashes and gurgles out a word. "RUINED!"

Mo skitters around collecting the white bricks and stockpiles them in the center of the room. I want to help, but I am in no condition. I push a few bricks toward Mo and shake my head. "What are we going to do?" I ask.

I expect him to come up with some positive statement or something. But all he says is, "I don't know. I don't know." He puts his head in his hands and runs frantically through the maze of fallen bricks.

I continue to push a few bricks to the center of the room. Mo crawls onto the pile and sighs. He grabs one of his poor, unfortunate whiskers and begins twisting. How is it possible for him to twist and twist and never have that thing come out? If I could, I would lift a brick and hand it to him. But even my good paw is simply not that nimble. I scoot a few more bricks with my nose over toward Mo.

Why did Clementine do this? It doesn't make sense. It's just mean.

I look at the pile of rubble on the floor. Then I have a wild thought. Actually, it might not be that wild after all.

"Mo," I say. "You can fix this."

"What? I don't know," he says.

"Yes, you can!" I ignore my aching foot and walk right over to him. I watch him twist that whisker, and I know his brain is plotting.

"Georgina is the architect, Elvis. I'm just a builder. I don't know how to do the design."

"I've sat here for the last four days watching you," I say. "If anyone can do this, it's you!"

Mo keeps twisting. Then, suddenly, *POP!* He holds that whisker between his thumb and forefinger and waves it in the air.

"Elvis, maybe you are right. Maybe we can rebuild! We must rebuild. We have no choice."

"Not we, Mo. You!" I say. "I can't build a Transamerica Pyramid. I can barely walk."

He marches around the room, and I already know I'm in for it. "You can do anything you put your mind to," he says. "And you're going to have to put your mind to this. I need you. We need you. Georgina will be back from Daddy's in two days."

He rushes over to the plastic palace and stashes that poor little whisker in a pile of fluff that probably contains other poor little whiskers. Then he scrambles back to me and starts barking out orders. "Get the book!" he says.

I know that Laverne is paying attention to all this because she's flipping and splashing and yelling, "THE BOOK! THE BOOK!"

Mo dances around in circles, and I can feel a tingling in my chest and the *thrum-thrum* of my heart. My leg throbs. My paw aches. My head spins. But I go to the bookshelf and I find the *Big Book of American Architecture*. I pull it out with my teeth, and I push it with my nose to the center of the room. I'm so exhausted when I get there, I think I might faint.

Mo opens the weighty cover with his delicate hands and flips through the pages with his nimble fingers. He finds the picture of the tall, pointy white building and taps on the page and looks up at me. "I'm counting on you, Elvis."

Even though I shake my head *no*, I say, "Where do we start?"

 # Chapter 11

I sit in front of Georgina's big book and study the photograph of the white skyscraper. It has a large base, but it gets skinnier and skinnier. "It's not like other skyscrapers," I say. "It's pointy."

"Yes," Mo says. "That's the pyramid effect."

Mo is good at putting the bricks in the right place. But connecting the bricks is harder. He pushes and pushes and strains himself until finally *SNAP!* Such a beautiful sound.

SNAP! SNAP! SNAP!

It's like a song.

After a while, Mo is out of breath, and I'm hardly helping at all. He leans over with his hands on his hamster knees and shakes his head.

"Are you okay?" I ask.

"I need to rest for a minute." He lopes over to his

plastic palace and climbs through the door at the top and then into a pile of fluff. He must be laying on his back, because his feet stick out and his toes twitch.

I contemplate the Transamerica Pyramid and try to pick up a brick with my good paw. No such luck. I lift one in my mouth and drop it onto the base of the structure. I press on it, but I can't get it to lock in place. So I whack it with my pink splint.

"Ouch!" The pain runs all the way up to my shoulder. But I think I heard the *SNAP!* I try again. And yes. *SNAP!* "Marvelous," I whisper. Then I laugh at myself for saying such a Mo-ish word.

I drop another brick into place on the base, but it's just too painful to do anymore snapping. And besides that, I'm hungry.

It's time for a snack. Thankfully, Georgina moved my food and water to the hallway after my accident, and I don't have to go downstairs. I take a few bites and go check the calendar. It seems like I've been here for a lifetime, but it is only July 9. There is a *D* in the box. Daddy. *D* today. *D* tomorrow and Sunday. *M* on Monday. That's when Georgina comes back. *M* is for Mommy. Of course it is. I'm not stupid.

I turn around at the sound of Mommy's *clippity-clopping.*

"Elvis," she says. She scoops me up like she does and presses me against her face and breathes her hot, dry breath on my neck. "Elvis, you might be more trouble than you are worth. But here we are. How is your little foot doing?" She kisses my splint and tickles the tips of my toes that are sticking out from all that pink. "Georgina is with her father for the weekend, and I'm leaving, too. But don't worry. Jasmine will be here in the morning to check on all of you."

"Where are you going?" I ask, quite clearly. Oh, right. Why do I bother?

Mommy sets me back down. Just then Clementine arrives and wraps herself around Mommy's ankles. But Mommy doesn't pick her up. She just pats her head and says, "good kitty," and tells us she'll be back on Monday morning.

Mommy *clippity-clops* down the hall to the stairs, with Clementine trotting behind her. Clementine yowls for attention, but Mommy just keeps going. When Clementine turns back to look at me, I pretend to be busy studying the calendar. But she knows I saw her. "Don't look at me," she says. I'm embarrassed for her. Maybe if you were a little nicer, Clementine. But no. You're not.

The front door slams shut. Mommy is gone. I don't understand the rules of this house. I long for the sound of Carly's cart and Etta's rumble. I wouldn't even mind hearing Rupert's complaints.

Friday, July 9, 6:37 PM

Mommy!

Which building did you used to work in?

When?

When you and Daddy both worked in SF.

405 Montgomery.

But they tore it down and made it into a hotel.

 # Chapter 12

When I wake the next morning, Mo is already working on the Pyramid.

"We've got a lot of work to do today, Elvis," he says.

I study the picture in the book and direct Mo when necessary. He snaps brick after brick into place. I take a chance and use my pink splint to *SNAP* one of the pieces in place. But the pain is still too much, and I decide I better hold off. I watch Mo scurry and *SNAP*. Scurry and *SNAP*. The Transamerica Pyramid is beginning to look like itself again. Sort of.

Suddenly, the whole house shakes as the front door slams downstairs. There is a mad scramble on the hardwood floors. And a huffing and panting. A beast has broken into the house and is coming upstairs to attack! The windows rattle, and my fur stands on end. I arch my back and—

"INCOMING!"

Before Laverne can even gurgle out a name, a gigantic canine flies into the room, barking and hollering as its furry tail whips from side to side like a weapon.

I hiss and spring back against the wall, then leap onto the chair and up to the bureau. Papers and trinkets scatter to the floor. My heart pounds in my chest. I try to grab ahold of the curtains with the claws of my good paw, but there is no way for me to climb up. I scoot onto the windowsill and try to save myself.

Laverne's bowl shifts on the bureau. A splash heaves over the side.

The beast stands there barking louder and louder.

Long strands of gooey slobber hang from the beast's mouth. It shakes its head, and the wet slop flies onto the chair and the bed and right past my face. A stringy piece of it lands on the Transamerica Pyramid and dribbles down the side.

I hiss again and call out for Mo while trying to hide behind the curtains.

"Holy habitat! The Transamerica Pyramid!" Mo says.

I don't know what to do, and I can't bear to see the skyscraper come crashing down again.

Just then, a long-legged girl with fancy twisted hair comes into the room. She grabs hold of the beast's collar and pulls it away from certain disaster.

"Bambi! Bambi! Stop it," she says. "You're going to scare everyone. Now SIT! STAY!"

The girl looks up at me and reaches in my direction. "Oh, my goodness. Elvis! You are adorable. And look at your little broken leg. Don't worry. Bambi won't hurt you." The girl lifts me off the windowsill against my wishes, and I hiss and pull back my head and try to push off from her. "I'm not going to hurt you, sweet thing. My name is Jasmine, and I am your friend."

I don't believe her for a second. But just in case she's for real, I say, "Then please get control of your dog." But she just *ooooh*s and *ahhhh*s and places me on the foot of the bed.

I immediately jump down, landing awkwardly on my bad paw, and crawl beneath the bed. I scoot to the far corner and watch the beast sniff around Georgina's room. It puts its snout under the bed and stares at me with its beastly eyes. It heaves a massive paw at me, so I swipe and hiss.

"Bambi! Leave Elvis alone. My goodness," Jasmine says.

The beast pulls back. I watch suspiciously as Jasmine walks over to the bureau and gives Laverne a few pinches of her food flakes. Then she leans down to Mo and lets him crawl into her hands. He scrambles up to her shoulder and behind her collar, and then up onto her head. Jasmine laughs and wiggles. Then she opens the latch to

Mo's plastic palace, and he crawls down her arm and goes inside. Mo fluffs his cheeks and twitches his whiskers as Jasmine adds nuts and seeds to his food tray.

"All is good in here," she says. "I'm going to refill your food and water, scoop the box, and check on Clementine. Be right back." She skips out of the room, leaving Bambi of Beastly Slobber sitting in the middle of the floor, right where Mo's pot of gold is supposed to be.

"Sorry about my entrance," Bambi says. "I didn't mean to scare you, little kitten. You can come out from under there. I'm extremely friendly. Some people think I'm overly friendly, but is there really such a thing as too friendly? I mean, who wouldn't want a whole pile of friendliness?"

I poke my head out and assess the situation. Bambi is a giant. Black and brown with a white neck, white paws, long hair, and floppy ears. And that tail. Back and forth, back and forth, back and forth.

"I'm working on my manners," Bambi says. "See how I'm sitting here as still as can be? It's pretty good. Well, except for my tail. It's hard to control. But when your human says sit and stay, that's what you're supposed to do. It's easy. Except when it's hard."

"You're a very big girl," I say, coming out from under the bed, still quite annoyed.

"I'm not a girl," Bambi says. "I'm named after a very famous prince, and he was a boy."

"Well, there was a Bambi at the shelter, and she was a girl," I say.

Mo skitters over and pipes in, "It's not a good idea to assume these things."

"I know," I say. Of course I know. Please.

"That's okay," Bambi says. "Part of my training at the shelter is to be patient and calm, especially when I meet someone new. Sometimes I have trouble, though, like I did a few minutes ago. I'm sorry about that. It's just going to take a while. That's what Jasmine says."

I jump at the mention of the word shelter. "Are you talking about the City Shelter of Care and Comfort?"

"Yes. It's an excellent school. I go every Tuesday from four to five P.M. Last week we learned about 'roll over.' It's so much fun. Your human says, 'roll over,' and you get on your back and squirm around. It feels good. And you get treats when you do it. You should—"

"Excuse me," I say. I can hardly stand all the babble. "Do you know how to get to the shelter?"

"Yes. Jasmine has a driver's license now. She has a car and everything. I'm supposed to ride in the back seat.

But I love jumping over the seat and sitting in the front. She doesn't like when I do that, and I'm trying to practice staying in the back. Jasmine says 'STAY' really loud. Sometimes it hurts my ears. I try to stay. I really do."

Bambi keeps rambling on and on, but the shelter! Maybe this beast is my answer.

"Bambi, do you think you could take me to the shelter?" I say.

"Yes. Of course. I—"

"BAMBI!" Jasmine yells from downstairs. "It's time to go."

Bambi jumps to attention and immediately charges out the door. I hustle to follow him, but my splint slows me down.

"When do you think we could go?" I call from the top of the stairs. But the beast is focused on Jasmine.

"COME, Bambi," she says. "SIT!" Bambi follows her commands and looks back at me and smiles. Jasmine looks up at me, too. "Goodbye, Elvis. See you tomorrow." They leave as quickly as they arrived.

My hopes for getting back to the shelter come crashing down again. Just like the Transamerica Pyramid.

I hobble back into Georgina's room, where Mo is at work.

"Hey," Mo says. "Does this thing look pointy enough?"

"No," I say. "Something is definitely wrong with it." Something is definitely wrong with everything. "Mo, do you think Bambi really could take me back to the shelter?"

"Anything is possible," he says. "But let's just take things one day at a time. Bambi and Jasmine will be back tomorrow. You can discuss it then."

"Okay," I say, and I can feel the hope in my heart picking up speed again.

 # Chapter 13

The next day, I am filled with energy. I almost wish I was a hamster on a wheel and not a kitten with a pink splint that weighs a thousand pounds.

I stray out into the hallway and check the calendar. Sunday, July 11.

When Bambi gets me back to the shelter, I'll find Carly and she'll tell me where Etta is. Maybe she's still there. Maybe she's with a family nearby. Maybe she is right on this very street. And Bambi can get Jasmine to take me to her. It's perfect.

"When will Bambi be here?" I ask Mo.

"Hard to say. Try not to worry about it. Now, let's get the spire installed on the pyramid. It's the final touch," he says.

I admire the tall, white structure. Wide at the bottom. Skinny at the top. But it's lopsided. Or something.

"Where is the spire, anyway?" Mo says.

"I don't know," I say. I sniff around the room looking for it. I check under the bed and behind the chair. Mo crawls along the floorboards, too. But no luck.

"Oh dear," he says. Then he grabs a whisker and begins twisting.

Laverne splashes out a warning. "INCOMING! DANGER!"

Clementine prances in and sits next to the pyramid.

"Clementine. Not again. Come on," Mo says.

"Ha! Don't worry about that," she says. "I've got better things to do than knock over your childish building blocks." She jumps up onto the bureau and sidles up to Laverne's bowl.

My body constricts, and there goes the fur on my back again. What is with this feline?

She inches closer and closer to Laverne's bowl and presses her eyes up to the glass.

"Clementine, what are you doing?" Mo asks.

"Just paying a visit to my aquatic friend."

Laverne swims into her cave.

"Please be careful," Mo says.

"Why do you have to do this?" I ask.

"Maybe I want to take a dip. Anyway, it's none of your business," she says. "You don't even live here, remember?"

My breathing gets heavy as I watch Clementine press her whole body up against the glass bowl. It moves just slightly, causing a tiny wave on the surface. I snap my tail and twitch my whiskers. I just know she is going to knock it over.

Mo paces and wrings his hands. "Clementine, please come down from there."

I slowly move to the chair next to the bureau. Clementine pulls herself up onto the rim of the bowl and dips a paw into the water and swirls it around. Watching this makes me twitch all over. When she starts to dip her other paw, like she's going to dive in, I can't take it any longer. I jump up to the chair, pulling the pink splint along with me, then bound up onto the bureau. I try the best I can to land gracefully on all fours, but my splint flies out in front of me on the slippery wood top, and I lose control.

My legs splay, and my whole body slides right into Laverne's bowl, sending it to the very edge of the bureau, where it teeters terribly.

"NO, NO, NO!" Mo shouts.

I watch as the bowl hangs on the edge and then tips over, falling to the floor in uncontrollable slow motion.

Laverne's home crashes and splashes and rolls across the rug. Water pours out. Blue pebbles scatter everywhere. Laverne's rock cave flies. And Laverne, poor

Laverne! I watch her flip out of the cave and flop over and over until she lands on her side, right next to the Transamerica Pyramid.

She gasps for breath and blinks slowly.

I tumble off the bureau, chasing after Laverne as if I could save the whole terrible disaster. "I didn't mean to do it," I cry. "I thought Clementine was going to . . . Clementine made me do this!" I say, and she did. She's terrible. She doesn't care about anyone.

"I did no such thing," she says from up above.

I'm at Laverne's side, with Mo bent over her, talking gently. "Laverne. It's okay. We're going to help you."

I can't imagine how in the world we are going to save her. Her mouth opens and closes like the howling of the hounds at the shelter. But there is no sound. Her eyes bulge and she stops blinking.

"Laverne, I'm so sorry. I'm so sorry," I say.

She doesn't say anything. Her feathery fins flicker, and she stops moving altogether. Her black eyes stare right at me.

"She needs water," Mo says. "We've got to get her to water."

"Yes," I say. How will we do that? Where is the water? I look around and think. "My water bowl. It's in the hall."

"That'll work," Mo says.

Mo cradles Laverne in his hands, carefully, preciously, and I don't know how he is going to walk on hind legs out to the hallway. It's not far for a human or for me, but for Mo, it's quite a distance.

"Get on my back," I say. "I'll carry you both."

It tickles as Mo crawls up onto my back and then settles in between my shoulder blades.

"You secure?" I say.

"Go, Elvis, go!" he says.

I walk slowly at first, and then move as fast as I can, considering my splint and my passengers. In a matter of seconds, I am in the hall at the water bowl. Mo climbs down and slips Laverne into the water with a lifeless *plip*.

Clementine slinks over and the three of us stare in shock.

"Breathe, Laverne. Breathe," Mo says.

She doesn't move.

Mo hangs from the side of the bowl and pokes at her. We wait.

My heart pounds in my chest, something I have certainly become accustomed to. I twitch my whiskers. I look at Mo and want to cry.

I did this.

I hang my head and stare at the floor. Georgina is going to be devastated. This is all my fault.

I know I'm not supposed to get it wet, but I dip my pink splint into the water and push Laverne around. Nothing happens. I splash the water. Still nothing. I close my eyes and drop my head.

Water dribbles down my face. I must be crying. Then—an astounding splash!

I look up and Laverne has righted herself and is swimming in circles.

"Look!" I say.

"Laverne," Mo says. "You're alive. She's alive!"

She splashes the surface. "Alive!" she says. "Alive!"

I laugh. A nervous laugh. A laugh of complete relief.

Mo chuckles. Then he laughs so hard his paunchy belly jiggles. Even Clementine lets out a sigh.

In that exact moment, I realize my leg is throbbing. Badly. All that leaping and jumping and landing added up to more pain. But I don't let on. Because now we have another problem on our hands.

"How are we going to get her back in her bowl?" I ask.

No one offers up an answer.

I wish Georgina was here.

 # Chapter 14

Laverne seems perfectly happy in my water bowl.

"You stay here with Laverne, and I'll see what can be done about the mess in our room," Mo says. "I've got some pebbles to gather. When Jasmine gets here, she'll make things right. Some things are beyond our scope of work, Elvis."

I wait by the water bowl while Mo does some clean-up. Clementine hangs around, too. But I'm so mad at her I can barely look in her direction. In the meantime, I try to bite away the wet, pink, sticky stuff on my splint. I manage to tear a few pieces, but I can't get to the aching part of my leg.

"You might want to knock it off with all that jumping around, Elvis," Clementine says. "It's just going to cause you more pain. And I know all about pain. What I used to do is—" She stops speaking abruptly, as if she wasn't talking in the first place. Which is fine with me, because the chances of anything useful coming out of her mouth are non-existent. She walks away. Please.

Moments later, the door slams downstairs and a whirl of noise rises up. Mo joins me next to the water bowl, and Clementine scoots back over.

Bambi thunders into the hallway, with Jasmine right behind him. Both of them come to an abrupt halt. I try not to look guilty. But I know I am.

"Hello, friends," Jasmine says before catching on. "Wait. What's going on here?"

There's no point in trying to explain any of this to a human. So, I just sit. Mo twists a whisker. Clementine grooms her orange patch.

"Oh my goodness," Jasmine says with exploding eyes. She crouches down on her knees and looks at Laverne. "How in the world did you get here? Mo? Clementine?" Maybe she won't say my—"Elvis?"

Mo and I follow Jasmine into Georgina's room, where she sets Laverne, still in my water bowl, on the bureau. Mo has piled up the blue pebbles, but Laverne's glass home and rock cave are where they landed.

"I don't know what you all think you're doing with Laverne, but this is not funny," Jasmine says.

"We saved her," I say, in a clear, loud voice, but Jasmine just shakes her head. She picks up Laverne's bowl and scoops up the pebbles and puts them inside, along with the rock cave. Then she walks out of the room.

"What happened?" Bambi asks, sniffing and wagging and slobbering all over everything.

"It was an accident," I say. "I didn't mean to do it, but I knocked Laverne's bowl and she fell out. She's alive, though. And I'm sorry."

"Whatever happened, Jasmine will fix it," Bambi says. "I know because one time I went outside when I wasn't supposed to and then I couldn't get back in the house and so I went for a walk down the street. I came back when I was hungry and tired and Jasmine wasn't mad or anything. She just hugged me and gave me my dinner. Everything was fine—well, mostly."

Jasmine comes back in the room with Laverne's bowl full of water and the pebbles and cave in place. "This water needs to come to room temperature before we put Laverne back in, otherwise she could go into shock. I'm going to leave this bowl right here while I check to see what other destruction you cats have caused. DO NOT TOUCH IT!"

I am so relieved that Jasmine will get this all sorted out before Mommy or Georgina comes home.

I don't want to be rude or disrespectful to Laverne, but I have to change the subject.

"Bambi, I have a question," I say.

"Okay," he says. "Questions are terrific. Especially if you want answers." Here we go with Bambi's rambling again. "I ask Jasmine questions all the time, but she doesn't exactly answer, and sometimes I think maybe she doesn't hear me. Why is that? She doesn't even have fur in her ears."

It's because humans don't listen, I think to myself. But I don't want to get into that right now.

"Bambi, can you really take me to the shelter? I need to find my sister," I say, approaching him calmly even though I am twitching madly on the inside.

"Oh, yes. I would love to. It's a magical place, like I told you before. When we get there, we can go right up to the front desk and try to sit still so we can get a biscuit. You have to sit very still, and you can't bark or anything, and don't even think of jumping or—"

"I KNOW IT'S A SPECIAL PLACE," I say a bit too enthusiastically. "I just need to know when we can go. It's urgent."

Bambi just says, "Oh," and sits there.

I wait, but he says nothing.

"We need to go now!" I say.

I don't know why he won't speak. I look at Mo and Laverne and Clementine, who is suddenly hanging around all the time. Finally, Bambi mumbles. Barely audible. A canine whisper, if there even is such a thing.

"I didn't really want to talk about this, but I may as well tell you," he says.

Mo scuttles over to get a better listen. Clementine butts in, too.

"I'm leaving Monday to go to camp. That's tomorrow," he says. "See, I didn't do very well in my class at the shelter. Now I have to go away for special training. I tried really hard, though, and Jasmine isn't mad, and she said that these things take time and soon enough I'm going to be very well trained and I won't knock things over or bark at everyone or run when I'm supposed to sit or sit when I'm supposed to come. It's just that sometimes I get distracted and I forget to concentrate, and then Jasmine gets frustrated and I cause problems and—oh, I'm so sorry."

"Okay, okay," I say. "So, we'll go when you get back. How long will you be gone?"

"Just two weeks." He pauses. "Then maybe two more after that. Then . . . it just depends."

The door to my heart shuts with a *snap-click*, just like the condos at the shelter. I try to keep my chin held up, but my head drops anyway.

"I'll take you as soon as I get back. I promise."

"Elvis," Mo says, climbing up my leg to get close to my face. "You need to rest. You can barely walk. You're not supposed to do anything for six weeks, right? It's all perfect timing. It is."

I'm so tired of Mo's perfect timing. I don't want to hear another word about it. My heart hurts. My head hurts. The very tip of my calico tail hurts.

My silent moment breaks when Jasmine comes back into the room. "Come on, Laverne," she says. "I'll bet you're ready to get out of the cat water. I look up and watch as Jasmine pours Laverne back into her home with a splash. She swims in circles and dives in and out of her cave. Her life is suddenly back to normal. Jasmine wags a finger at all of us. "You people be nice to Laverne," she says. Then she tells Bambi it's time to go and walks out.

Bambi nudges me on his way out. "The weeks will go by in a jiffy. That's what Jasmine says."

Mo chuckles. "Ha! Jasmine called us people. That's funny."

I am in no mood to laugh. It will be a lifetime before Bambi comes back for me.

I look up at Laverne, safe in her home, and I can't deny that I am so relieved. I only wish I could feel the same about Etta. I miss Etta. And I have no idea where she is.

 # Chapter 15

Georgina finally comes back on Monday morning. Mommy, too. I hear her *clippity-clops* downstairs.

"I missed you, Elvis," Georgina says.

She picks me up and walks me around with her, gently scratching my head as she checks on Laverne and then sits down next to Mo's palace. Mo comes out and scrambles onto Georgina's leg and then up onto her shoulder.

It is strange and wonderful to be missed.

The three of us sit together for a few minutes, and I wonder if Georgina has any notion of all that occurred in her absence. Can she tell that the Transamerica Pyramid came crashing down? And that Mo and I rebuilt it? Did Jasmine tell her about Laverne? There is so much to discuss, and apparently no words to use.

Clementine pokes her head in the doorway, and Georgina calls to her. But she doesn't come in.

Mo crawls to the floor, and Georgina sets me down, too. She studies the Transamerica Pyramid. I watch as her smile slowly leaves her face and she wrinkles her brow. Oh shoot.

"What happened here?" she says, looking from the pyramid to me to Mo.

"Uh-oh," I say to Mo. "She knows."

Mo scrambles over to her and shimmies up her leg and into her lap. I go to her, too, and give her a headbutt.

She looks confused. But she's not mad.

She takes apart the top of the Transamerica Pyramid and starts re-snapping pieces together. Occasionally she looks over at me with questions in her eyes.

Oh, how I wish I could tell her. "We should have done a better job," I say to Mo. I should have helped more. But how?

"We did our best, Elvis, considering the circumstances," he says. He grabs a shiny, white brick and hands it to Georgina. She puts it in place with a *SNAP*. Mo hands her another, and then another, and pretty soon, all that is left to connect is the long, thin spire.

"Where is the spire?" Georgina says. She shakes her head in confusion. I look around the room, trying to figure out how to solve this problem.

I see Clementine in the doorway. She motions to me. "Elvis," she calls.

"What do you want now, Clementine?" I have had enough of her antics to last a lifetime.

She nods in the direction of the bookshelf.

"Oh, now you want in on the reading?" I say.

"No! Just . . ." She nods again. Then she sighs. And smiles a weak smile. "Elvis, follow me." Clementine comes in and walks over to the bookshelf. I am right behind her. She nods again, and I follow her gaze.

I look at the bookshelf, and there, resting on the bottom shelf, is the spire. I slink over and nudge it with my nose. Push it with my paw. I look up at Clementine. She looks me in the eyes, like she might even be sorry for what she did. Then she slinks out the door. I pick up the spire in my mouth and walk over to Georgina and drop it in her lap.

"How did you know that's exactly what I needed?" she says. Her eyes sparkle when she says it.

"Because I'm listening to you," I say.

Georgina scratches behind my ears. I don't know how to tell her the things I want to tell her. But none of that matters right now. I'm helping Georgina. For real. I lift my chin and purr.

Georgina spends quite a bit of time tinkering with the skyscraper. She fixes it just right and clears a spot for it on her shelf, right next to the Sears Tower. "I should have put this up on the shelf before I went to Daddy's," she says. She places a picture in front of it. It's Georgina. With a human man. It must be Daddy. They are standing in front of a white building. I can't tell if she's smiling.

The rest of the day we page through the *Big Book of American Architecture*. I see almost every letter of the alphabet, arranged in fancy ways to make words that humans read. Reading and writing. It's all so easy for humans. So why is listening so hard for them?

Suddenly, Georgina picks me up. "Elvis, do you want to see something? Mo, you, too. Come on."

Georgina leans down and Mo crawls into her cupped hands. She puts him on her shoulder, and he holds onto her collar. With me tucked under one arm, she climbs through the window and steps us all out onto a ledge enclosed with a rail. Then up, over the rail she goes, hoisting herself onto the roof. I've never been up this

high. We're on top of the world. And, as an added bonus, we are in the out-of-doors.

A cool breeze sweeps through my whiskers and rustles my fur. Peeking out from under Georgina's arm, I can see all sorts of things. Streets, cars, trees, rows and rows of houses. Off in the distance is water. So much water. I can't imagine how many water bowls worth of water. And something that reminds me of the connecting ramps in Mo's palace.

"Look at that red structure, Mo," I say.

"Ha! That's the Golden Gate Bridge. It's world-famous," he says.

On one side of this bridge, there are grassy peaks. On the other side, there are buildings, standing shoulder to shoulder on a hilly landscape. I can see a pointy white skyscraper that looks just like—hey! "Is that—"

"Yes. It is," Mo says. "That's San Francisco. And you're looking at the real Transamerica Pyramid, right there in the middle. Do you see the spire at the top? Isn't it marvelous, Elvis?"

I can't believe it. The real Transamerica Pyramid. "It looks exactly like ours, Mo," I say.

"Yes, sir. I told you we were talented."

"Mommy and Daddy used to work right near the Pyramid. In San Francisco," Georgina says, as if she might have actually been listening to us.

We stand there, on the top of the world, and look across the water in silence. The sun illuminates the grand bridge. Bold red glitters on blue waters. A white pillowy puff of cloud floats overhead. It's beautiful.

Slowly, my gaze returns to what is right in front of me. I look down at the streets and houses that seem to go on forever. "Etta is out there somewhere," I say.

"Yes," Mo says.

"But we can't know for sure," I say. "I'll never know if I can't get back to the shelter to find out."

"You'll know when the time is right," Mo says.

Georgina looks at me suddenly. Straight into my eyes. And I wonder again if she understands what I am saying. She scratches me behind my ears and smiles, and her eyes sparkle. "It's time to go back inside," she says.

Back in Georgina's bedroom, Mo heads to his palace, mumbling on his way. "Just because we were outside doesn't mean you should get any wild ideas about trying to leave again."

The window is shut, so it doesn't matter anyway. I'm stuck. And I know it.

I am about to tuck myself into the pile of wrinkled clothes under the bed when Georgina takes me into her arms and presses her head against mine and whispers in my ear. "I wish we could go on our family vacation. That's what families are supposed to do together."

"I want to be with my family, too," I say.

Georgina kisses the top of my head and sets me on the floor. She reaches for her bin of LEGOs and says, "New York City."

Before I know it, Mo is front and center twisting a whisker.

"New York City is where all the best skyscrapers are," he says.

Georgina sits down on the floor next to us.

"I bet we're going to build them all," Mo says.

I look from Mo to Georgina. Her brow is furrowed, and her lips are pressed together. Mo scrambles up her arm and onto her shoulder and clasps her collar. "The Flatiron Building!" he shouts. "The Chrysler Building! The Empire State Building!"

"That sounds like a lot," I say.

"We can do it," Mo says.

Georgina cups Mo in her hands and lowers him to the floor. She dumps out two bins of plastic bricks, and Mo dives right in. She presses two gray bricks together, *SNAP*.

"New York City," Georgina says again. And I get the

feeling that there is something very important about the skyscrapers there. I don't know what it is, but I see Georgina's determination and Mo's enthusiasm, and it occurs to me that there is so much in this world that I don't know.

Monday, July 12, 8:58 PM

Daddy. Thanks for the fun weekend.

Here is a pic of my T-pyramid.

Hometown favorite! Glad we got to see it in person.

You're going to talk to Mommy about New York City, right?

I will talk to her.

But we need to be realistic, G. ♥ ♥

I am being realistic.

♥ ♥ ♥

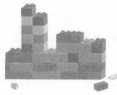 # Chapter 16

The next few weeks go by very slowly. I am resigned to healing and waiting and hoping and trusting. Nothing in my life has ever been so hard. One day I will find Etta, and she will find me, and we will be together. But it's not going to happen anytime soon.

My leg improves with each passing day, and soon my food and water are moved back downstairs and I am getting around just fine. However, I take the stairs one tread at a time with carefully placed paws, just in case.

I'm used to the schedule now as Georgina regularly goes to Daddy's. It's easy to keep track, thanks to the calendar in the hallway. I don't like it when she's gone, but when she returns, my ears perk up and I feel—I don't know—alive.

I love the sound of the front door opening and shutting and Georgina's footfalls as she runs up the stairs and into our room. I am always ready for her to scoop me up and tell me in her soft, cozy voice about how much she missed me and how happy she is to see me. She does the same with Mo, patting his tiny hamster head. It seems like she would lift Laverne right out of her bowl if she could, and kiss her feathery fur. She even snuggles Clementine, who has been hanging around more and more.

And what comes next is always wonderful. Georgina sits on the floor with Mo and me and builds skyscrapers in the middle of the room.

Mommy usually comes in and tries to convince Georgina that she should have a playdate. A human friend. But Georgina doesn't need humans. Why would she, when she has us? Also, humans don't listen, so what's the point?

We build the Flatiron Building and the Chrysler Building one after the other.

Georgina tells us what it would be like if she and Mommy and Daddy went to New York City. "We'd see all these skyscrapers in person. And we'd take our pictures in front of them and we'd look up to the tip-tops and feel like ants. And we'd walk everywhere together, like we did in Chicago. With me in the middle."

When she talks about it, her voice is low and slow, and it almost makes me sad.

When we build the Empire State Building, I am fascinated. Georgina reads about it from her *Big Book of American Architecture*. The building is a symbol of America's ability to dream. After all, it was built during the darkest days of the Great Depression. We don't talk too much about what the Great Depression was. But everyone knows it was depressing. And as for dreaming, I am a big fan. I love that the people who dreamed up the idea for the Empire State Building wanted to make it the tallest building of its time. While Georgina and Mo build, they chat about colors and design.

Georgina talks about how the top is in a style called art deco, like the Chrysler Building. I tell Mo that the Empire State Building is a combination of the Sears Tower and the Transamerica Pyramid.

"How so?" Mo asks.

"See how it's a square," I say. "Like the Sears Tower. But its skinny at the top and has a spire, just like the Transamerica Pyramid."

"You're becoming an aficionado," Mo says.

"A fishy what?"

"An expert. That's what happens when you pay really close attention to something. When you study something that interests you and try to learn all you can about that something, eventually you know things that others have never considered."

I spend time thinking about this. To be an expert sounds good. I am interested in skyscrapers, sure. But I am more interested in letters. The way that humans use letters to communicate. I want to understand letters, too. I wish I had that alphabet book of Carly's. Then I could communicate with Georgina and tell her that I need to find Etta. If I could tell her clearly with letters, she would understand me.

When I tell Mo about this, he hops up onto the bookshelf and starts poking around. And miracle of miracles, he taps his hamster fingers on a skinny book jammed on the second shelf.

"Here's an alphabet book, right here," he says. "There is no reason you can't study your letters now. It's a worthy task."

I yank that book out with my teeth and Mo flips the pages for me. Sure enough, all those letters are right there, in their perfect order.

I don't get it, though. How do they work? I see the letters, but I don't understand the patterns.

"This is hard," I say to Mo.

"Life is hard," Mo says. "That doesn't mean it's not worth trying."

I think about this for a minute. "I know," I say.

Georgina and Mo build. I help with what I can, of course. But mostly I study the letters.

"*X*," I say, thinking of Etta and me.

"*X* is in the word *expert*, Elvis," Mo says. "You can hear it right in there."

"You know, I'm an expert on Etta," I say, as Mo and Georgina finish with the Empire State Building.

"Oh?" Mo says.

"Of course. Etta loves to pretend to be an *X*," I say.

"To be an expert, you need to know a little more than just that," Mo says.

"Etta treads in her sleep," I say. "And her rumble is soft and sweet. And her whiskers twitch when she's hungry." I try to picture her sleeping right now. I wonder what her bed looks like. Does she have a warm pile of blankets to sleep in? What does she eat for dinner? Does she have roommates like Mo and Laverne? What about a human friend?

Is there a sad and grumpy feline in her house like Clementine?

When I add up all that I know about Etta, I realize I don't know much at all. I don't even know where she lives. I feel stuck all over again and stare at the *X* in my alphabet book. The only thing *X* really means to me is that the day is over. Done with. Crossed out.

Georgina suddenly bursts with information about the Empire State Building. "It was finished in record time," she says. "Four and a half floors per week—we were much faster than that! It took a total of seven million hours. That's with six thousand workers. It says right here it was a multiethnic work force."

"What does that mean?" I ask Mo.

"It means when everyone is from different backgrounds," Mo says. "Like all of us."

"That's what I thought," I say. But it sounds ridiculous. I'm a cat from a shelter. Mo is a hamster in a plastic palace. Laverne lives in water. Georgina is a human who lives in two houses. And yet here we are.

Mommy comes into the room and stands with her hands on her hips.

"We finished it, Mommy," Georgina says.

"I can see that," she says. "You certainly are focused, Georgina. That's such a positive trait that will serve you well in life."

"Mommy, did you know that an airplane flew into the Empire State Building?" This certainly gets my attention.

"You mean the Twin Towers—the World Trade Center," Mommy says.

"No, I don't."

"Yes, you do. 9/11. We've discussed this before."

"Look, Mommy. Read this right here." Georgina points to a page in the *Big Book of American Architecture*, and Mommy reads aloud.

"On July 28, 1945, at 9:49 A.M., a B-25 bomber accidentally flew into the seventy-eighth and seventy-ninth floors of the Empire State Building. Because it was a Saturday, fatalities were minimal." Mommy looks up and says, "Wow! I had no idea. I have never heard anything about this in my life."

I look over at Mo, shocked. An airplane crashing into a skyscraper. That's terrible. I can't believe that would happen. Mo scampers over to the book to look at the picture.

Georgina continues. "It says that the building didn't come crashing down. It was open for business the very next Monday. But, Mommy, the Twin Towers came crashing down. Why did the Empire State Building stay in place? I don't understand."

"9/11 was different," Mommy says. "It had to do with the size of the airplanes. And all that gasoline."

"You saw the Twin Towers in real life," Georgina says.

"Yes, I did. That was a long time ago."

"It's not fair that we can't go to New York! Why can't we go?"

"Georgina, we've discussed this."

Georgina sighs and drops her head. "I need a picture, Mommy. From when you and Daddy visited. Just before 9/11. I know we have one. I've seen it before."

"You remember everything, don't you, Georgina?" Mommy says.

I finally have to ask Mo. "Why does she keep saying those numbers? Nine and eleven?"

"It was the date of the tragedy," he says.

I walk over to Georgina and give her a headbutt. She lifts me into her arms and snuggles me. But no one says anything else about those numbers.

 # Chapter 17

"Bambi should have been back by now," I say to Mo while he's shredding part of an egg carton.

I amble into the hallway to check the calendar. The letters that used to be at the top, J-U-L-Y, have been replaced with A-U-G-U-S-T. I know all these letters, of course. And Mo already told me that the month after July is August, so, technically, I know what those letters spell. And we're already halfway through it!

It is Saturday, August 14. There is a big *D* in the square, which makes perfect sense since Georgina left for Daddy's house yesterday. I come back into our room and tell Mo the date.

"It's been more than four weeks," he says.

"I knew it!" I reply. "Where is Bambi? He was supposed to come back for me."

"Maybe they made him stay at camp," Mo says. "Poor pup."

"Poor pup, nothing," I say.

"Elvis, you know that the chances of Etta still being at the shelter are slim. It is unlikely," Mo says.

I know this is true. Of course I know it. But who on earth would leave their sister and never try to find her again? "Why would Bambi make a promise and not keep it?" I say.

Laverne flips and splashes. "INCOMING! DANGER!"

Clementine prances in and scowls right into my face. "Don't you know you can't depend on a dog?" she says.

"A promise is a promise," I say, turning my head away from that annoying feline.

"Dogs are not in control of their own lives. They love being told what to do—all that *sit*, *stay*, *shake* garbage. If you want something important done, ask a feline."

"What? Are you going to take me to the shelter?" I laugh at the thought of it.

"Yes," she says, licking at her orange patch. "If it's the only way to get you out of here. Then, yes. I'll take you to the shelter."

"You don't even know how to get there," I say. Please.

"I know a lot more than you or that ratty mouse give me credit for," she says.

"Clementine," Mo says. "We give you credit for a lot of things. We just wish you'd be a little friendlier."

"THAT'S WHAT I'M DOING RIGHT NOW!" she yowls. "Besides, I have my own reasons for going."

I cock my head sideways and snap my tail. "How do you know where the shelter is?" I walk closer to her. "Why didn't you say something earlier?" I am suspicious. And twitchy.

"None of that matters, you fluffy imp," she says.

"When can we leave?" I ask.

"As soon as we get that wretched pink thing off your leg."

Mo scrambles up to Clementine, holding his hands out to her face. "This isn't a good idea, Clementine. You haven't thought this through."

"It's a great idea," I say. "She wants to help. It's a miracle!"

"I've thought it through plenty," she says. "Let's get busy. Mo, get your nasty, gnawing chompers ready. We're going to need them."

 # Chapter 18

Mo is reluctant. But I beg and beg and beg. Like a dog. It's embarrassing.

Mo gives in and gnaws at my splint. I sit very still.

"Can't you go any faster?" I say.

"This isn't exactly a piece of cardboard. I don't know what the material is, but I will say that it's easier than plastic. I once chewed through a plastic container of almonds. I'd never tasted almonds and was thoroughly intrigued. But plastic! It's terrible."

Mo continues chewing, but also takes frequent breaks to talk about plastic like a plastic know-it-all. It makes me twitch. Every moment that I am not on my way to the shelter is, once again, a waste of time.

"I love my plastic home," Mo says. "But plastic has taken over the world. The material itself is miraculous. I mean, look at these LEGOs. But you can never get rid of it. Thankfully, the LEGO people are testing organic materials, like corn and wheat. Isn't that marvelous?"

"Mo, please concentrate," I say.

"Once I got to the almonds, there were plastic bits everywhere. I opted to reuse and recycle. I fashioned them into an artistic sculpture. It's displayed right there on level three." He points to his palace.

I squint my eyes, and sure enough, some crazy artsy thing is sitting in the corner on one of his platforms. *A* is for appreciate art.

Mo continues gnawing, and Clementine pulls with her teeth. It's not fun to be the subject of this project, but eventually my paw is free. And then my whole leg. I hold it up. It looks terrible, all skinny and sickly. But I've never been so happy to see my own leg.

I bite and pluck at the matted fur and lick and groom to try and make it look respectable.

"Not the most attractive leg I've ever seen," Clementine says.

"Be careful when you step on it," Mo says.

I gently place my foot on the floor and tap twice. "Feels strong to me," I say. I take a step and put my total weight on the newly revealed paw. I slip and fall over.

"Holy habitat! Elvis, be careful!" Mo scampers around me, pulling on a poor, unsuspecting whisker.

"Mo, I'm fine," I say. "I just need to get used to it. It's not a problem."

"There's nothing to worry about," Clementine says. "We'll be taking this journey slowly anyway. I'm not exactly a cheetah. Now, come on. Let's get downstairs. Mommy is down there somewhere, and it's just a matter of time before she opens the front door." Clementine turns to me. "Are you coming or not?"

"We're going right this minute?" I say. I want to go. I've been wanting to go for weeks. So why is my head spinning?

"Of course," Clementine says. "You too, Mo! Get a move on."

"Me?" Mo says. "Oh no, I'm too old to venture out into the wild. I have reservations about the two of you as well."

I lean down and nudge Mo with my nose. He chuckles and tips over. But I suddenly have an ache in my stomache. "Georgina might not like the idea of all of us leaving."

"On the contrary," Clementine says. "She'd want us all to stay together."

Hmmm? Maybe she would. The more I think about it, the more I realize I don't want to leave without Mo.

Mo stands and brushes his hamster hands down the sides of his round, fluffy body. He starts to reach for that whisker. He's considering going. I know he is. If he starts to twist, it's as good as a done deal.

"Listen," he says. "A lesser rodent like myself has no business on the streets with two felines." But as he says it, his fragile little wrist begins to turn. I glance at Clementine, who rolls her eyes. Then, *voila*! He twists, and I am so relieved.

"Oh, thank you, Mo! Thank you!" I say.

"I didn't say anything," Mo says.

"You didn't have to. Now climb on board. You can ride between my shoulder blades. It's first class up there, Mo. First class!"

Mo crawls up my good leg and over my shoulder. He nestles into his comfort spot.

"This is against my better judgement," he says.

"But it's still a good decision," I say.

"Traveling with a fluffy imp and a ratty mouse," Clementine says. "Who would have thought?"

Who would have thought is right. Traveling with

Clementine? But I don't say anything negative. Instead I say, "It's a multiethnic adventure."

Laverne splashes out a goodbye and good luck, and then we hobble down the stairs, hide behind Big Ben, and wait.

 # Chapter 19

The ticktock of the clock reminds me of a heartbeat again. Or maybe that's my own heartbeat I feel.

Mo's grip on my scruff is tight. I can feel his tiny nails clutching on, and it tickles. But the three of us wait without saying a word. I have questions, that's for sure. There is a part of me that is still not sure I can trust Clementine. How does she know how to get to the shelter? Why would she want to go there anyway? Maybe she's playing a horrible trick on us.

I am about to speak when the door flies open and Mommy marches in with her arms full of grocery bags and walks straight to the kitchen.

"Now!" Clementine yells.

We dart out the door and skid into place next to the flowerpot. I haven't been in the out-of-doors in quite a long while. The smells. The sounds. The air itself. Fantastic!

"There's no time to lollygag," Clementine says. "We have to get on our way right now so Mommy doesn't spot us."

"It really is easy to get out of this house," I say.

"Of course it is. You should know that by now," Clementine says.

"Where to?" I say.

"Just follow me. We'll take the sidewalks until we have a reason to stay out of sight."

Looking over my shoulder at the house, I wonder if we'll get back before Georgina returns from Daddy's.

I walk next to Clementine with a tiny little limp and a whole pile of hope.

The air is chilly, but I feel alive. That whitish-gray fog stuff hangs in the air. It's fluffy, like Etta. And also like the fluff in Mo's plastic palace. Ha!

Our pace is slow, with me just out of my splint. We hobble and wobble our way down the street.

"How are you doing up there, Mo?" I ask.

"I'd rather be indoors," he says. "This is not my favorite thing in the world."

"You're my emotional support, Mo. Thank you for coming."

We turn the corner, and there are so many cars. They zip and zoom past, and I wince at the memory of my accident. "Kind of dangerous out here," I say.

"Like I told you before," Clementine says. "Life is dangerous. But if you want to get what you want, risks must be taken."

Mo whispers in my ear. "I hate to say it, but she's right. No risk, no reward."

"I know," I say. I feel the risk loud and clear turning flips in my stomach. I just want to hurry up and get to the reward.

A car slows down next to us and a woman calls out the window, "Oh no! Little lost kitties. Here kitty, kitty." The car stops and the woman starts to get out.

"Leave us alone," Clementine hisses. "This way, Elvis."

I follow Clementine into a plant with long, thin stems that have tiny purple buds at the ends. So sweet smelling.

We duck there for a few moments, then make our way to an alley, where we hide behind a garbage can.

"This alley is actually a shortcut. We'll be fine," Clementine says.

"I hope so," I say.

It's a thin gravel road jammed with parked cars and garbage bins and an odor that stings my nose. A cold wind picks up and ruffles my fur. Dust blows in my eyes and I blink rapidly, trying to clear the itch. "How much further?"

"We're close. When we get to the coffee shop up ahead, we go right, and then we walk past the pet store, and then it's two more blocks."

"A pet store," Mo says. "Oh dear."

"I thought pet stores were your motherland?" Clementine says.

"It's true. I was born in a pet store." Mo says. "But let's not talk about that right now—we have goals and objectives."

Yes. Goals and objectives.

"Clementine, do you go to the shelter often?" I ask.

"Maybe," she says. "It's not really any of your business now, is it?"

Mo digs into my neck with his claws. But I'm curious.

"Why haven't you ever mentioned it before?" I say. "Do you have littermates? A brother? A sister?"

"Shut your yapper," she says.

"I'm just curious," I say. "Geez."

"Well, you know what they say about curiosity and cats."

"Of course I know," I say. But I have no idea, and that makes me even more curious. I don't pester her anymore. I can't help but think that Clementine has a family out there somewhere.

Clementine looks up and nods at what is in front of us. "This is Kal's. It's a coffee shop. Now follow me to the back. It's snack time."

We enter a narrow space around the side of the building. There is a door there with a tiny bell mounted to the wall, right at our height. Clementine headbutts the bell.

"Well, isn't that convenient," Mo says. "I think I might like a bell at my place. I'm putting that on my project list."

In no time at all, a strange-looking girl opens the door. She has drawings on her arms and neck and metal clips in her nose and ears and on her eyebrows. She looks like she is being pinched.

"Yikes," I say.

Clementine snaps her tail at me and says, "Oh, stop

it, Elvis. This is Pearl." Clementine purrs seductively and slinks around Pearl's ankles, which are also covered in drawings.

"Hi, sweet baby," Pearl says. "I see you brought a playmate today. How wonderful." I feel Mo burrow into my neck, and I don't think that Pearl sees him. That is until she leans down and scratches my chin. "Oh wow! Is that a hamster? Holy moly." She reaches out to touch Mo, but he burrows in. "Okay, little fella. I'll leave you alone."

Pearl pats the top of my head and then reaches into her pocket and produces a small bit of something. She gives a piece of it to Clementine and a piece of it to me. She even puts a tiny morsel on her finger and presents it to Mo, who accepts it, I think. Not that I can see him at this point.

I sniff the small bit and decide to give it a try. I can't place the taste, but it is delicious.

"*Du fromage!*" Mo says. "Cheese."

Pearl gives us each another bit, and it makes my tummy sing.

After a few minutes doting on us, Pearl bids us farewell. "Be careful out there. I'm a little nervous for you all," she says, and heads back inside.

I'm not nervous. I just want to get there.

Clementine gives me another nod, and I follow her back out to the main sidewalk and past the pet store.

"How'd you get so popular?" I ask, as we continue down the block.

"Humans can't resist my charm," she says.

"All humans except Mommy," I say, walking faster to keep up. Then I immediately want to take it back. "I'm sorry. I didn't mean that."

"Don't talk about her!" Clementine says. "And stop asking me so many questions."

Mo leans over my eyebrow whiskers again and whispers, "Careful. She's sensitive and—" But I jolt to a sudden halt because Clementine has stopped, and I can't believe my eyes. The most beautiful building ever constructed in the history of the world is standing in front of us, just across the street. Three glorious stories of red brick. Wide windows. Old Glory, shifting smoothly in the breeze at the tip-top. It should be in the *Big Book of American Architecture*.

I whisper in awe. "It's the City Shelter of Care and Comfort."

"So it is," Mo says.

"I told you I'd get you here," Clementine says. "All we have to do is cross the street."

I look at all the cars, and my stomach churns. I start to shake, and that uncontrollable mewing comes out of my mouth in small bursts. I lift my paw slowly and place it timidly onto the black surface of the road.

"Wait!" Clementine yelps. "We have to wait for the light to turn green. Are you crazy?"

"I know. I know," I say. Of course I know. Please.

"You didn't know, and I'm here to tell you," she says.

"Please, just be careful," Mo says.

A car pulls up along the sidewalk next to us and of all things in the world—it's Bambi! He's barking and barking and barking and drooling out the window.

Before I can grasp what is happening, Jasmine jumps out of the car and runs around to us. "What are you doing here? Oh my goodness." She grabs Clementine with one arm and me with another, and Mo clutches my scruff for dear life. "Mo?" Jasmine says. "Oh my goodness. Is Laverne here, too?" She looks around as if we'd brought a traveling fishbowl with us. Then she opens the back door and practically tosses us in.

Bambi jumps from the front seat to the back, squashing us all. "I'm so happy to see you," he says. "Are you going to the shelter? Because we just came from the shelter. I finished at camp and I'm in a new class. I'm doing so much better. I do exactly what Jasmine tells me to do, and I almost never get in trouble. Isn't that great?"

I knew this day was too good to be true.

"You blew it, Bambi," Clementine says.

"Now, everyone just calm down," Mo says. "Bambi, we were trying to get to the shelter."

"You never came back to take me," I yelp. I want to cry. But I don't even know what good it would do. I've done everything I can do to try to get to the shelter. And in my heart, I know that Etta isn't even there anyway. It's all been a big, huge waste. And I hate everything about all of it.

To top it off, Bambi is just pitiful sitting there between us. I don't want to talk to him. I don't want to even look at him. Or anyone.

"I'm trying to do what Jasmine says." He flings his slobber around and tries to bite it out of the air. "I just want to be a good dog. That's all I want. I'm sorry."

I crawl onto the floor of the car and curl into a ball. Mo is still hanging on to my scruff, and I wish he would just get off of me. But it doesn't matter anyway, because we are already back at the Pemberton's house, and I am never going to get to the City Shelter of Care and Comfort. Never.

PART 2

Mommy, I've gone through every box here, and I can't find a picture of you and Daddy in New York City. It was in an album.

Will you PLEASE look in your stuff?

Ok. I will look.

Your phone is supposed to be for emergencies only!

This is an emergency! 😠

 # Chapter 20

Jasmine brings us to the front door. To say that Mommy is surprised is not saying much.

"How on earth did they get downtown?" she says. "And Mo, too? This is outrageous!"

"I have no idea, Mrs. Pemberton," Jasmine says, setting Clementine on the floor and handing me to Mommy. She pulls Mo out of her pocket. "I'll take him upstairs for you," she says. I stand there unmoving and unhappy.

"Clementine, thank god you're okay. And Elvis, where is your splint? This can't have been good for your leg." Clementine circles Mommy's legs, and for a minute, I think Mommy might pick her up. "It's a good thing you made it back before Georgina gets home. I wouldn't want to upset her. I just wish things were normal around here."

Mommy always wants things to be normal. I don't know what that means.

I pass by the kitchen and don't even stop for water before slogging up the stairs to our room. Mo is back in his plastic palace making fluff, I guess. Not that I care. I just want to go to sleep. So I crawl under the bed and look for my pile of wrinkled clothes. But it's gone. I close my eyes and try to disappear.

When I wake up again, I don't know where I am. I don't know what day it is. I don't know what the point of anything is at all.

I hear Mo on his wheel and snap back to the reality of this stupid house and poke my head out from under the bed.

"You slept a long time," Mo says.

"Whatever," I say. "I'm done with these shelter shenanigans."

Mo stops and steps off his wheel. I'm not looking at him, but I know that he has climbed through the door at the top of his palace and is skittering over to me.

"I know this feels like a setback," he says. He does that Mo thing where he puts his hands on my cheeks and looks into my eyes. I consider popping him into my mouth and putting an end to all of this.

"I am destined to be here. Without Etta," I say.

"That might be true," he says. "But remember what I said about focusing on the positive?"

I don't want to hear about Mo and his positivity. I shake Mo off and crawl back under the bed. "I need to be alone," I say. But that pesky hamster follows me under the bed.

"Life is mysterious," he says. "We are not always meant to know why things happen the way they happen. Sometimes the information we want is not available to us."

"STOP, MO! JUST STOP IT! You don't have any idea what it's like to be forced to live somewhere without your family. No one in this house could possibly understand. I live in one house. My sister lives—I DON'T EVEN KNOW WHERE SHE LIVES. It's not normal for families to be all split up. That's what I'm saying. And I wish someone would under-stand what I'm talking about! No one knows how I feel."

I look up at Mo. Standing beside him is Clementine. "Have you even been paying attention around here?" she says.

"What?" I say. "I always pay attention." What is she talking about? Oh, who cares.

"INCOMING! THE KID!"

Oh, Laverne. Sometimes I wish she would just go jump into the San Francisco Bay.

Georgina is back from Daddy's.

She finds me under the bed. Her smile is enormous. Her arms are outstretched. I wish she wouldn't do this.

"Elvis, come out, come out. How is your leg? I heard about your adventure. I can't believe it. You are so brave," she says. Her eyes sparkle, and I can't help but approach her.

I look at Georgina and speak as clearly as I can. "I have a sister," I say. "Her name is Etta. She's gray, with white paws. She treads in her sleep and likes pretending to be an *X*, and I miss her so much. All I want to do is find her and get everything back to normal."

Georgina looks into my eyes. Is she listening to me? Can she hear what I'm saying? She lifts me into her arms and gently strokes my withered leg. And that's when it hits me. Georgina lives in two houses. Clementine—

she's separated from someone, I'm sure of it. Mo, born in a pet store but here now. And me and Etta. We're all scattered everywhere.

This life is a rotten mess. And yet, all I want to do is bury myself in Georgina's warmth. It's confusing to miss Etta so much but also to want to be here right at this moment.

Georgina sets me on the foot of her bed and whispers in my ear, "Elvis, I'm so glad you're home."

 # Chapter 21

A couple of weeks go by, and we don't do a lot of building. Mommy takes me to the vet to make sure my leg is okay. The vet says I am healing just fine and don't need a new splint. I already knew that. Please.

Mo spends most afternoons working on projects in his plastic palace. He occasionally skitters over to the bookshelf and taps on that alphabet book. But I'm not really that interested right now. I've started to hang out a little bit on the foot of Georgina's bed. I like how I can see everything in the whole room from here. And Georgina is gone a lot. She has swimming and the library and something that Mommy calls, "back-to-school shopping."

"She needs new shoes," Mo says.

"I know," I say. Humans always need new shoes. I'm not stupid.

When Georgina is in our room, she spends most of her time on her bed staring at a certain page of *The Big Book of American Architecture*. The very first page, I think. Then she closes the book and stares at the ceiling and then looks at that page again. But she doesn't read aloud to us. And it makes me wonder what she's thinking. She doesn't tell us anything. I don't know why.

Then one evening, August 25—it's a Wednesday—Georgina suddenly stands up and makes an important announcement. One that breathes new life into all of us.

"We are starting on the World Trade Center today—the Twin Towers," she says, holding her chin in the air. I think she means business.

I hear a few plips in Laverne's bowl and see her two bulging eyes staring through the glass.

Mo suddenly pops up next to me. All ears.

"Mommy and Daddy saw the real Twin Towers in person. When they were young. They went on a trip to New York City and saw the World Trade Center. They took a picture there, too. Mommy even thought about becoming an architect back then. But she became a finance person instead. Anyway, none of that matters. The only thing that matters is that New York City is where our family started. The World Trade Center towers are very important to our family."

Georgina reminds me of Carly—it's like she's telling us a story.

"I never thought a skyscraper could be that important to a family," I say to Mo. "It's not like it was their home."

"Sometimes unexpected things feel like home," he says. I never really thought about that either. But maybe it's true. Mo crawls up onto my head and stands on my eyebrow whiskers. Such a hamster.

Georgina is excited. I can tell. She is also serious. She breathes deeply and takes *The Big Book of American Architecture* and sits on the floor and looks through the pages with focused eyes. Mo and I watch as she stops on the page with the Twin Towers. The tall, skinny buildings that stand side by side. Two identical structures. Then she flips the page, and I see a very interesting skyscraper. It's got so many sides to it. It's not a rectangle or a square or even a pyramid. Weird.

Mo scrambles off my head and over to the book. "That's the Freedom Tower. It's part of the *new* World Trade Center," he says.

"There's a new World Trade Center?"

"That's it right there," Mo says, tapping on a page in

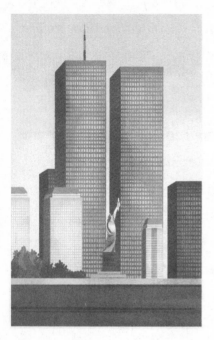

the book. "After the Twin Towers fell, they had no choice but to rebuild."

"That's a lot of work," I say.

"Yes. They demonstrated resilience and fortitude."

"Resilience and fortitude. That's exactly what I was thinking," I say. "What does that mean again?"

"It means you can never give up. When they rebuilt the World Trade Center, a message was sent to the whole world."

"What message?"

"That no matter what, we're going to keep going."

"Oh," I say.

Georgina studies her book, and I can tell that she's making a plan. I'm glad, I guess. But right now, I'm just so tired. I don't even bother to jump down and crawl under the bed. I just stay up there with Georgina, tuck my paws under my head, and close my eyes.

I don't think about anything at all.

 # Chapter 22

I'm half asleep. Dream-thinking about those towers. And those people who rebuilt there. I hear a splash and open my eyes.

"INCOMING! MOMMY!"

I jump out of my fur. Lavern's warnings are helpful—and also startling.

Mommy walks into the room and stands with her hands on her hips. Then she pets her hair tail. "What are you all up to?" she says.

"Mommy, we're starting on the World Trade Center today. The Twin Towers."

"That's wonderful, Georgina. Do you want to invite a friend over to help you? I hate to see you spending your last bit of summer vacation in your room all by yourself."

"But I'm not by myself!" Georgina stands and spreads

her arms out toward me and Mo, like she's presenting us to Mommy for the first time ever. "I have lots of help."

"I think Mrs. Lin's daughter likes LEGOs, too. We could invite her over."

"Mom! This is my project. It's special to me. I don't want help from Mrs. Lin's daughter."

"Of course it's special, Georgina. But a little human interaction every now and then can't be that bad."

"I have human interaction. With you! And I'd have more if Daddy still lived here."

At this moment, I feel like someone opened the window and let in the shivering San Francisco fog.

Georgina turns and marches over to her LEGOs and dumps out a bin of gray ones. Clementine tries to get Mommy's attention by circling her legs and yowling.

"Georgina, don't get upset. Come on, now," Mommy says, all droopy like one of those Basset Hounds.

Georgina turns to face Mommy. Her eyes are damp. This makes me nervous. "Everything is ruined," she says. "Daddy's gone. We're not going to New York City, and I can't even find that photo album." Georgina's negativity is just like Rupert's.

I headbutt Georgina on the ankle. I want her to calm down. I want her to sit and work quietly on our skyscrapers. But that's not what she does.

"There's a picture, Mommy," she says. "Of you and Daddy in front of the Twin Towers. From your trip to New York all those years ago. You've told me the story a million times. You and Daddy went to New York City that summer to sing with your choir at Carnegie Hall. It was the summer right after you graduated from high school. It's in that photo album. You used to call it the album of your love. You were standing in front of the Twin Towers. Only a few weeks before they fell. Don't you remember?"

"Of course I remember," Mommy says.

"Well, I need that picture! Where is that photo album?" Georgina's face is red. Her nostrils flare, and she shakes. I've never seen her this way.

"Is this about 9/11, Georgina? It's upsetting to all of us, especially since we're coming to the anniversary. People are talking about it." Mommy crinkles up like she's in pain.

"Yes!" Georgina cries. "And I need that picture."

Georgina paces around the room like a lost chihuahua, and Mommy follows her, trying to get her to calm down.

"Georgina, I wish you would tell me what this is all about," Mommy says. She reaches out, but Georgina is having none of it. She stomps out into the hallway and opens the closet.

I watch from the bedroom door as she pulls out boxes and crates and plastic containers, tossing papers and clothing and old toys everywhere. A doll with painted lips and a broken arm lands right next to me. Mommy picks it up and holds it tightly to her chest, squeezing it to death—just like she did to me when she first held me on the Fourth of July. Is she crying?

"I'm sorry, Georgina. I don't know where the album is."

"The Twin Towers are gone forever, and you don't even care about that picture."

"Of course I care, Georgina. We have other pictures. Surely we can find one for you," Mommy says.

Georgina runs past me and back into her room. She picks up the *Big Book of American Architecture* and holds it in front of her. "I need that picture. I'm going to build the Twin Towers, and that picture goes with it, like this one of us in Chicago goes with the Sears Tower." She points to her shelf. "And that picture goes with the Transamerica Pyramid, the place you used to eat lunch with Daddy when you both worked in

San Francisco. Daddy used to go to your office and meet you for lunch. He told me about that. He said you would sit right there next to the Transamerica Pyramid and eat dim sum from Chinatown."

Mommy looks like she will collapse at any moment. She doesn't even grab her tail of hair. "Oh, Georgina," she says.

Georgina swings the book around and throws her head back and squeezes her eyes closed. "Why did you even buy me this book? And why did you write that in my book? Why?"

"What?" Mommy says.

"You wrote it in my book," Georgina says.

I am confused by this and don't know what they are talking about.

Georgina opens the book to the first page, the one she kept staring at before, and reads aloud. "'*For Georgina, Build a world of your own choosing.*' That doesn't make any sense!" she says, through gasps and chokes. "How am I supposed to do that?"

Georgina drops the book on the floor and falls to her bed, burying her face into her pillows, sobbing.

The one thing I do know is that I can't take it anymore. I jump up onto the bed and give Georgina a soft

headbutt. She doesn't reach for me. I lick her arm and nuzzle her shoulder. Even Clementine jumps up there, shocked and staring. Mommy tries to sit on the bed next to Georgina, but Georgina won't look at her. They are both sniffling, and I can see Mommy's hand reach out to stroke Georgina's hair. But she pulls it back and finds Clementine instead.

"Georgina," she says softly, so softly that I perk my ears and listen hard. "Sometimes things happen that are out of our control, and it's okay to be upset. But there are some things we *can* choose. We can choose how we react when things change. We can choose what to do next. Life is still good, Georgina, even when it feels unbearable."

Georgina doesn't look up and doesn't speak. Mommy reaches for her again. And this time, she pets Georgina's hair. She leans down and kisses her head. After a few minutes, Mommy looks at us and leaves.

Mo crawls up onto the bed and over to Georgina's pillow and sighs. "If there was ever a time when Georgina needed our help, it is now. Building the World Trade Center is necessary. Georgina needs to do this, and we need to help her."

Mo is right. I feel it in my heart, and I want to be a part of it. "I'm going to help," I say. "In whatever way I can."

"That's admirable," Clementine says, licking her orange patch. "But I'm just going to sit here." Lick, lick.

"In the sun." Lick, lick.

"And watch." Lick.

I think that's the least-rude thing Clementine has

said since I've been here.

We all wait for Georgina to come back to life. And when she does, after a long while, she sits down in the middle of the room and begins sorting bricks. Occasionally, a sniffle escapes from her exhausted body, and she gasps and hiccups and bounces slightly. It reminds me of the sad hounds at the shelter who just want someone to stop and tell them that they are loved.

I headbutt Georgina's hip and nuzzle her side. "I am here for you, Georgina," I say. "I love you."

Georgina reaches out to me and Mo. She looks up at Laverne. I can tell we are just what she needs.

Well, us and skyscrapers.

 # Chapter 23

Mommy doesn't come back in our room for the rest of the day. She leaves Georgina and us to do what needs to be done. And through the process, there is so much interesting information to learn about the Twin Towers and the World Trade Center. It's more than just two identical buildings standing side by side.

"It was like its own little city," Georgina says, wiping her sniffly nose. "It consisted of seven buildings. It had a train station and stores and a barbershop and restaurants, a police force, nine chapels, and it's very own zip code."

"What's a zip code?" I ask Mo.

"It's a number that identifies a geographical location—it's part of the address. If anyone asks you yours, tell them 94611. That's where we live."

"When they built the Twin Towers," Georgina says,

"they wanted them to be the tallest buildings ever. Taller than the Empire State Building. Of course, the Sears Tower ended up being taller than all of them, but still. They used two hundred thousand tons of steel. The outer steel walls were built to resist 150 mile-per-hour winds. And the engineers calculated that if a plane accidentally flew into the towers, they wouldn't fall down."

"But they fell down, right?" I say.

"That's because humans don't know everything," Clementine says.

"Also, it wasn't exactly an accident," Mo says.

"Someone flew into the Twin Towers on purpose?" I say.

"Sadly, yes," Mo says.

That makes no sense whatsoever.

"Why, Mo?"

"That's something we might never understand," he says.

I certainly don't get it.

Georgina keeps talking about the details of the construction. I could listen to her voice all day long. The way she talks about the architect, the location, all the workers. It's like she's an expert. But nobody ever explains why someone would fly an airplane into a skyscraper.

The construction goes on for several days. Mommy doesn't ask about playdates. The A-U-G-U-S-T is gone from the calendar. Now it says S-E-P-T-E-M-B-E-R, and Georgina says that summer is almost over.

Mo and Georgina work hard to finish the Twin Towers and the smaller buildings around it. I do what I can, but mostly I'm there for emotional support. It's almost done, and I can see how it does look like a little city—like when we climb up on the roof and look at San Francisco. I watch the two of them working. It's like they speak the same language. But everyone knows hamsters and humans can't communicate.

"Mo," Georgina says, "the north tower needs to be slightly higher than the south tower."

"Oh, right," Mo says, looking over at me. "The real one was six feet taller. A good architect is always proportional." Mo helps Georgina add one more layer of bricks to the north tower.

"Mo," Georgina says, "let's install a tightrope between the two towers."

"Like the one Philippe Petit walked across," Mo replies.

It's like they are talking to each other. Or something. Usually, they're so quiet.

Georgina goes to her desk and pulls out a ball of string and cuts a piece. She pulls a brick from the top of the north tower and one from the top of the south tower. Then she presses each end of the string into the open grooves of the bricks and snaps them back into place. It takes a couple of tries for her to get the string tight enough. But as soon as it is right, Mo climbs the south tower and steps onto the tightrope.

"This is marvelous," he calls to me. "Can you believe a man actually walked between the two towers? A thousand feet in the air?"

"Mo, be careful. You could fall," I say. And why would a human do that?

"It's hard to be down when you are up!" he shouts. "That was the motto when they built this thing. Ha-ha!"

Mo stays on all fours and scoots out a few steps. He scoots out a little farther.

"This makes me nervous," I say.

"I don't even need a balancing pole," he says.

I watch Mo move carefully on that rope. It sways, and for a moment, he hangs upside down. I can hardly stand it. I close my eyes.

"He's had plenty of practice balancing in high places," Clementine says. I didn't even realize she was here. "Rodents are nimble, Elvis. Especially Mo."

I know that she must be right. There is no one in the world like Mo. No one as smart. No one as brave. No one as wonderful. Just like Georgina. But thinking about how wonderful Mo is makes me worry even more. "Mo, please come down."

I'm watching him again, and he is chuckling as he makes his way across the rope.

Finally, he is safe on the top of the other tower. He stands on his hind legs and pumps both fists in the air and shouts at me. "Holy habitat!"

Georgina claps and reaches out her cupped hands. Mo climbs in, then skitters up on her arm to her shoulder, where he grabs onto the collar of her shirt. They are both so proud.

Laverne splashes twice. "INCOMING! MOMMY!"

Mommy comes into the room. She doesn't put her hands on her hips. Or even pet her tail of hair. She is calm and quiet. Come to think of it, I didn't even hear any *clippity-clopping*. Clementine immediately nuzzles up to Mommy and slinks around her ankles. "Georgina, pretty soon you need to start getting ready to go to Daddy's." She walks around the room picking up clothes and putting books back on the shelf. She stops for a moment and stares at the Twin Towers and the whole World Trade Center city. "Wow!" she says. When she dips to pick something off the floor, Georgina leans to stay out of her way. When Georgina reaches to add a brick, Mommy stands back. She furrows her brows and doesn't move. I can see them avoiding each other's eyes. But I see Mommy's eyes, and I think that she might start crying all over again.

Georgina finally speaks up. "Mommy, I want to take Elvis to Daddy's this weekend. He's never been to my other house, and he deserves to go."

I instantly perk up. What? Go to Daddy's house? I've never even thought of that.

"Oh," Mommy says. "Do you really think that's a good idea?"

"Yes!" Georgina says without looking up.

"Well, you can ask Daddy. He's coming in for a few minutes. We're going to talk about the school-year calendar."

I sneak over to Mo, who is back in his plastic palace snacking on a sunflower seed. "Why would Georgina take me to Daddy's?" I ask.

"Because she wants to share her world with you," he says.

"But I thought *this* was her world," I say.

"Georgina's world is much bigger than just this room," Mo says. "You should talk to Georgina about it."

"Mo, we don't speak the same language." I snap my tail in frustration. "You know that."

"You don't have to speak the same language to understand each other," Mo says. "You have common ground." Mo scurries over to me and does his Mo thing.

He reaches up to my cheeks and holds my face, and with his black eyes piercing through me, he says, "Elvis, communication doesn't always come from words. It can come from actions. It's what we *do* together that connects us. That's how we learn to understand one another. That's where the magic happens."

Mo trickles away and admires the towers. What is he talking about? Actions? Magic? Ugh.

"Elvis," he says, "now tell me what you think about the Twin Towers. They are my favorite skyscrapers ever. I love how they are two buildings that belong together."

I look at the twins. A brother and sister, standing shoulder to shoulder, the tightrope stretched between them. They are tall and skinny and surrounded by an array of other structures. Like a family of buildings. They were supposed to withstand any sort of destruction. But they collapsed anyway. It doesn't make sense. And what does Mo mean by common ground? My head hurts.

Mo turns to me and grabs a whisker. "Do you have a favorite building, Elvis?"

A favorite building? I don't know. But I humor him, as always. "Of course," I say.

"Well, tell me!" He starts to twist that whisker.

The Twin Towers are marvelous, to use Mo's famous word. I really do think that. I look up at the shelf where all the other skyscrapers sit, tall and proud. They are impressive for so many reasons. I look them over and consider all their admirable qualities. But the truth is that my favorite isn't up there. It's probably not that famous. And it certainly isn't very tall.

"My favorite building in the world is the City Shelter of Care and Comfort," I say.

Mo grins. And, thankfully, he lets go of that whisker.

"Nice, Elvis," he says. "Very nice."

 # Chapter 24

Daddy arrives a few minutes later.

"INCOMING! DADDY!"

I'm not going to say anything to Mo, but I'm curious about going to Daddy's—to see another part of Georgina's world.

I look up and see a man standing in the doorway. Daddy! He's not as tall as I thought he would be. He has graying hair, like Mo. But his smile is just like Georgina's. The two are a matched set. Like the Twin Towers—except that Georgina is shorter, like the South Tower.

Daddy leans down to Georgina and gives her a hug. He looks at the Twin Towers and inspects them closely. "This is incredible, G," he says. His eyes sparkle like hers. And now that they are at the same height, they look more and more like the Twins.

"Daddy, this is my best project."

"Your mother told me how important it is to you. Who helped you?" Daddy runs his finger along the rope connecting the two towers.

"Mo and Elvis, mostly," she says. "They've helped me with all my skyscrapers." My heart flutters when she says my name.

"That's so nice of them," Daddy says.

"I really wanted that picture," Georgina says. "From the album. But the album is officially lost, I guess."

"It'll show up eventually, G," Daddy says. "Wow. I really can't believe you made this."

Georgina points out all seven buildings of the World Trade Center. Daddy sighs. And I think he might cry. The Twin Towers make everyone in this family cry. She shows him her other skyscrapers.

"These are beautiful, and I am so proud of you," he says. "I can't believe you built all these just by studying your book—without any of those LEGO kits! They're so intricate."

"I'm ten. I don't need kits anymore. Remember?"

"I know," Daddy says. "What you've accomplished is spectacular."

Daddy kneels and reaches for me. "You must be Elvis," he says. I don't mind at all when he scratches behind my ears. "It's great to meet you in person. Or, in kitten, as the case may be. I understand you've been through quite a lot."

"I have," I say. But before I can tell Daddy more, Clementine butts in.

"Hello, Clementine. My sweet Clementine," Daddy says. "How I've missed you, gorgeous girl." Daddy picks her up and snuggles her and pets her, and she loves every second of it. Clementine looks down at me, and, the truth is, I can't deny that I am happy she is getting some attention.

"Daddy," Georgina says, "can Elvis come with me to your house this weekend?"

"Oh, I'd love to have him, G. But the apartment rules and all."

Daddy holds Clementine and strokes my back at the same time. I love how he calls Georgina "G." It's a great letter. I decide right then and there that I want to go to Daddy's house.

"Daddy, no one would have to know. We can sneak him in, and it would only be until Monday morning. Please, Daddy!"

"It wouldn't be fair to Clementine, would it?"

"She can come, too."

I look at Clementine, who is now as full of hope as I am. But then I look at Mo. Mo needs to come, too.

"It will be an adventure, Daddy," Georgina says. "They won't make any trouble. Think how much fun we'll all have. Mommy doesn't care anyway."

I watch the way Clementine responds to Daddy. She is tucked into his chest, and her eyes are closed.

"I really want to go," I say, and I give Daddy a good, strong headbutt to make my point.

Daddy is quiet for a moment. Then he looks around Georgina's room and says, "Okay. But only this one time. Go ahead and get their supplies. You're going to need to bring a bag of food and some kitty litter. I can't believe I'm allowing this."

"Thank you, Daddy!" Georgina hugs Daddy, and Clementine and I get in on the snuggle.

I look over at Mo, who is busy in his plastic palace. "You're coming with us, right?" I say.

"No, no," he says. "Don't worry about me. I'm not a good traveler, remember? I need to rest, anyway. I'm tired from all this construction work."

I don't want to go anywhere without Mo, but maybe just this once.

Georgina untangles herself from our embrace and twirls out of the room, leaving Clementine and me wrapped in Daddy's arms.

"I'm not gonna lie, Clementine," he says. "I have missed the heck out of you. We're going to have a wonderful weekend." Daddy carries us both out of the room.

"Goodbye," Mo calls out. "I'll be here when you get back."

In a matter of minutes, I'm back in my cardboard carrier with Clementine tucked in beside me. I'm excited, but I shudder in the same moment. Every time I've been shoved into this box, something terrible has happened. I realize right then just how hard it is to be a cat in a human world.

"I don't know what we're in for," I say to Clementine.

"Expect the unexpected," she says.

"The unexpected is always distressing," I say.

"Not always," she replies.

Spending the weekend with Clementine is truly unexpected.

So is her optimism.

 # Chapter 25

Everything is different at Daddy's house.

For one thing, when you walk through the front door, you are practically in the kitchen. A short stroll from there is the bedroom and the bathroom. There aren't any stairs at all. And not very many hiding places. But it doesn't matter, because I don't feel like hiding.

There's a cushy-looking sofa against the wall, and a picture of Georgina. In the picture, she's smiling with sparkling eyes, the way she looks when she's working on skyscrapers.

I jump up onto the sofa, careful not to put too much pressure on my bad paw. But, come to think of it, my paw feels great. And that makes sense, because according to the calendar, it's been more than six weeks.

From atop the sofa, I have a view of the whole place. It reminds me of being in the condo up front at the shelter.

"Okay, G, you'd better set up the litter box right away. You can put it in the hall next to the laundry closet. And go put your backpack away," Daddy says.

Georgina tucks her backpack into the corner next to a large, puffy chair. She pours the litter into a small box and sets it in the hallway, if you can even call that a hallway—it doesn't really go anywhere.

"Where's Georgina's bedroom?" I ask Clementine, who is nosing around in the kitchen.

"How should I know," she says. "I've never been here."

"I don't think she has one," I say.

Clementine saunters over to where the litter box sits and peers around. "Not much privacy," she says.

I laugh.

Soon enough, all four of us are close and comfortable on the sofa. I'm on Georgina's lap and Clementine is on Daddy's lap. When Daddy gets up to get snacks, he takes Clementine with him, tucked under his arm. Back on the sofa, he settles her exactly the way she was before, like it is all perfectly natural. Smooth and easy. That's how it feels. No one jumps or jolts or strains or stomps. It's what Mo would call "heaven on earth." Even with Clementine. She's different at Daddy's.

I listen to the soothing sounds of Georgina and Daddy's conversation.

They talk about everything and everyone. They talk about school starting soon and how that makes Georgina feel—nervous and excited. They talk about how quickly summer has gone by. They talk about skyscrapers. And they talk about what happened in New York City way back when.

"Your mother and I sang at Carnegie Hall," Daddy says. "We were so young."

"I know. I've heard the story before, Daddy."

"We made grand plans back then. We were barely eighteen. Your mom thought about becoming an architect. Did you know that?"

"I know that, too, Daddy. You're acting like I didn't pay attention to you all those times."

"I just want you to know, G, that you are so much like your mother, in so many ways. You're headstrong, Georgina. That means you are brave and determined. And that makes me so happy and so proud."

"Why did everything have to change?"

"Because life changes. But it doesn't mean that we're not still a family."

"I know that," Georgina says. "But it was better before."

"In many ways, yes," Daddy says. "But our futures our bright, G." Daddy hugs Georgina, a tangled, snuggled hug, with Clementine and me in the mix. It feels so good.

"So, G," Daddy says. "What are you going to build next?"

"I don't know," she says. "I'm still deciding."

"So many choices. How about the Eiffel Tower?"

"No. I'm thinking of something else."

Georgina jumps up, and I leap to the arm of the sofa. She hustles out of the room and comes back with a bucket of LEGOs.

"More LEGOs?" I say to Clementine.

"They're taking over the world," she says.

"Okay, G. Before you get going, let's make dinner, then you can start on your next masterpiece."

Georgina and Daddy go to the kitchen, and I watch them chop and slice and make things sizzle.

It still does not make any sense to me why humans want to live in two houses. It doesn't seem right that a family is not all together in one place. I try not to think about

Etta. But I can't help it. I just wish I knew where she was. It would make me feel so much better. Just to know.

I jump up onto the back of the sofa and knead on the velvety blanket folded there. My whiskers tickle the edge of the curtains around the window. I nose my way between the lengths of fabric and twist and turn my neck, stretching and arching and trying to relax. With my eyes closed, I press my face up against the glass, like I used to do in our condo at the shelter. The sun spills around me, and the warmth of the glass spreads throughout my body.

I open my eyes and look out into the backyard, expecting to see squishy grass or an oak tree with rambling branches or maybe a squirrel traveling along the top of a fence. But there is no yard. Not like at Mommy's. All I can see are cars, lined up, row upon row. No swing set. No bird feeder. Nothing interesting.

Past the cars, I see a fence enclosing them. What is that beyond the fence? I jolt up, snap my tail, and prick my ears forward and chirp. It's something I recognize.

A sight for sore eyes.

A dream come true.

Of all the luck!

"Clementine! Get over here!" I yowl.

"What's caught your fancy now?" she says.

"You're not going to believe it!"

Clementine saunters toward me in slow motion, and I want to leap out and drag her over here. "Hurry up!"

"I'm coming. A lady must take her time if she wants to arrive in style," she says. Clementine hops up onto the back of the sofa, and, panting softly, she takes a moment to groom her orange patch and smooth down her fluffy cheeks.

"Look out the window, will you?" I stand on my hind legs and reach up to the curtains and pull them open. "Look at it!"

"Calm down, you fluffy imp," she says. When she spots it, she straightens up and gasps. She looks at me and is speechless. Not one sassy word. We look at each other, and finally, Clementine borrows a phrase from Mo and whispers, "Holy habitat."

"Holy habitat is right," I say.

"Who knew that Daddy's house was so perfectly located?"

We both stand on our hind legs and reach our paws up onto the glass, like a couple of *Xes*. I'm so excited that I cannot contain myself. I yowl and yip and cackle and chirp and make every imaginable sound.

Georgina rushes over to the sofa and pulls the curtains away, revealing a clear view out the window. "What do you two see here? What is making you so excited?"

I calm myself and take a deep breath and make my very best effort to speak clearly, without any extra mews or squeaks or overly anxious chatter. "It's the City Shelter of Care and Comfort. It's right there!"

 # Chapter 26

I look into Georgina's sparkling brown eyes and repeat slowly and clearly what I just said. "It's the City Shelter of Care and Comfort. Right there."

She tilts her head and squeezes her shoulders around her neck. "What are you trying to tell me?" she asks.

"I'm trying to tell you that the shelter is right there. I can go find out what happened to Etta. Maybe I can find Etta." I twitch my whiskers, snap my tail, splay my claws and even hiss, but just for effect. "Georgina," I say. "Please listen to me. You can take me—us—there. You can!"

"Elvis, you are looking at that building, aren't you?" she says.

"YESSSSSS!" I yowl.

"That's the shelter, Elvis."

"I know," I say. "That's what I'm trying to tell you."

Daddy walks over. "You know that Clementine came from the shelter, too, G. She was awfully sad-looking. But I loved her immediately. And I brought her home to your mother."

My eyes find Clementine's, and she looks as hopeful as I feel.

"I know, Daddy. And that's where Mommy got Elvis. I think he is excited about seeing it."

"He certainly is making an awful racket. I think he's a bit out of sorts being here at the apartment. He might be scared, too."

"No," I say. "Georgina is right. I'm not scared. I just need to get to the shelter." I stand on my hind legs and reach out for Georgina. She takes me into her arms and snuggles me.

I look down at Clementine. "Why can't they understand what I'm saying?"

"Because humans are flawed. I've told you this a thousand times." Clementine headbutts Daddy in the arm and mews loudly.

"Old girl. What's the matter? Do you not like it here?" Daddy says.

"I love it here," Clementine says. "I wanted to come live here with you when you moved."

"You'll feel better in the morning, Clementine," Daddy says. "These two need some time to adjust, G. It's all overwhelming."

Georgina's breath warms my neck as she speaks. "Elvis, I know you're excited. I wish you could tell me what you need."

"I am telling you," I say. "I'm trying my best."

"Daddy," Georgina says. "Something important is happening with Elvis and Clementine. Something we need to figure out."

"They're just unsettled. Let's call it a night. Tomorrow, things will be clear. We have a big day, too. All these LEGOs will magically transform into something spectacular."

"Okay," Georgina says. She lifts me to her face and looks right in my eyes. "I love you, Elvis. I love you, too, Clementine. We'll figure this out tomorrow. I promise."

 # Chapter 27

I stare out the window at the shelter until the sky is so dark that I can't see anything. I'm going to find a way to get there. It's going to happen. And Clementine, I don't know . . . she needs to go there, too. For some reason. That's good enough for me.

My hope is mixed with frustration because I don't know how to tell Georgina. It's impossible to talk to her. Humans don't listen. I know this to be true. I've studied the alphabet. I know the whole thing! Well, mostly. But it's not doing me any good.

I'm all itchy. I can't stop twitching.

Daddy moves Clementine and me off the sofa and sets us on the floor. He takes all the cushions off and pulls on a handle that I didn't even know was there. And right before my eyes, the sofa turns into a bed. Georgina and Daddy arrange the sheets and blankets, and

Georgina crawls under the covers. I hop onto the newly transformed sofa and nestle in at her feet. Clementine hops up there, too, and Daddy kisses us all good night.

Clementine takes some time to lick and preen. I pull on that place between my toes that always gives me trouble.

After a while, slow, soft breaths come perfectly timed from Georgina's open mouth. Her chest rises and falls and provides the soothing rhythm that I love. In the meantime, I yank a bit of matted fur out from between the toes of my healing paw. I lick the tops of my paws and brush the damp fur over my eyes and ears. There's a spot on the back of my head that I can't reach. I stretch and contort but I can't clean the out-of-reach spot.

Suddenly, Clementine is there. She preens and cleans and cares for the places that I cannot get. It is truly unexpected.

"Thank you," I say, surprised.

"It's the maternal instinct," she says.

"What do you mean?" I ask.

"I mean, a mother just knows what needs to be done," she says.

"Whose mother? Is this a guessing game?"

"Me," she says.

"What do you mean, you?" I say. "Are you somebody's mother?"

"You're not the only one who has been separated from their family."

Clementine? A mother?

I stare in shock at Clementine, who diverts her eyes and groans. I don't even know what to say. But a few words fall out of my mouth. "That's why you want to go to the shelter. To find your kittens?"

"You are a smart one," she says. "But yes, that is why."

I hesitate for a moment, then I ask, "How many kittens did you have?"

"Four."

"What happened to them?"

"My hope is that they were adopted into nice families. That they are happy and healthy. That's all a mother wants for her children."

"Are they all together?"

"Most likely not. But I guess you know about that."

I drop my head, but I can't stop flicking my tail.

"When they found us, they took my kittens from me—I couldn't care for them. I was too weak." Clementine hides her face. "They were adopted. Like you, Elvis. But it took several weeks before I could be brought out of the back room. I was worn out and sick. It seemed like no one would want me."

It all makes perfect sense now. "That's why you were part of the Second Chance Club, right?"

"Yes. But Daddy found me and brought me home to Mommy. He gave me to her. I'm hers, and she was supposed to love me. Daddy wanted her to love me. He thought that new love would fix things for everyone. It didn't work. And he moved out."

"I know Mommy loves you, Clementine. Of course she loves you," I say.

"The plan didn't work. You can't force love." Clementine sinks deeper into the bed covers. "I wanted to live with Daddy. But the apartment rules. We're not even supposed to be here now."

"Clementine. We're going to find a way to the shelter. I'm going to find out where Etta is, and you're going to find your kittens." I know this is true. I feel it in my heart.

Clementine stands and yowls a sad, low yowl. "You don't understand, Elvis. My kittens aren't kittens anymore. It's not realistic to think that I'll ever see them again. It's just the way the world is."

I feel Clementine's emptiness inside myself. "Clementine, sit back down." I gently nudge her. To my surprise, she does what I say and curls up next to me. She tucks her paws under her head and closes her eyes.

I nuzzle Clementine's side and scoot in close. I wrap my tail around her body. I take a deep breath and release the contents of my lungs. Slowly, Clementine's rumble begins. The vibration calms us both. Even yesterday, I could not have guessed that it would be like this.

As I lie next to Clementine, I picture her kittens. Four kittens. I wonder what they look like. Was one of them a calico like me? Was one of them gray with white paws like Etta? Does one of them have a little orange patch like their mother? Do they like to pretend to be *X*es?

I know that I must find a way to get us both to the shelter to find answers. I must try. It's a matter of life and death.

Suddenly, an idea strikes me with tremendous force. Like a 180-mile-per-hour wind. Or a 6.9 magnitude earthquake. It hits me with the power of a New York City skyscraper!

"Wake up, Clementine," I say. "Wake up!"

Clementine lifts her head. "What is it now, Elvis. Can't you see I've had enough? Can't you see I'm tired of all of this?"

"I know," I say. "But I have a plan."

Georgina.

I know you're asleep at Daddy's.

I found the album.

I love you.

 # Chapter 28

I pop up and jump down to the floor. "Come on, Clementine. Trust me on this one!"

"I don't want to leave my nest."

"Just wake up and get down here. But don't make too much noise. We don't want to wake Georgina or Daddy."

"Sheesh! You're so demanding." Clementine tumbles down to the floor and slinks over to me. "What do you have up your sleeve, you fluffy imp?"

"Fluffy imp is your way of telling me I'm special. Admit it!"

"Yeah, yeah! So what? Now, out with it!"

"Georgina's LEGOs, Clementine," I say. "I don't know why it took me so long to figure this out."

"What about the LEGOs? Don't tell me you're going to build the Eiffel Tower as a gift to the humans."

"The Eiffel Tower. Please. You and I are going to build the City Shelter of Care and Comfort."

Every bit of me twitches, flicks, and snaps. I spy the bucket of LEGOs and pounce, tipping it over and spilling the shiny bricks all around me.

"You're out of your mind," Clementine says. "We are not mousy rats like Mo. Our toes are not nimble, Elvis. You will be disappointed."

"Clementine, this is the simplest building ever constructed. It's not made from nine bundled tubes. It's not a pyramid. There's no art deco designs to deal with. And it doesn't have matching towers. It's only three levels, made with red bricks and Old Glory flying at the top. How hard can it be?"

I dig through the LEGOs scattered on the floor. I push them all around, separating out the red ones. There aren't that many, but that's okay, because there are enough to make a small replica of the shelter. "Clementine, see if you can find something that looks like a flag. For the top."

"But why are we doing this?" she asks.

"Because it's our common ground. We're doing it for Etta. We're doing it for your kittens. We're doing it because we have resilience and fortitude and we are never giving up."

I look Clementine directly in the eye. Without a hint of sarcasm or negativity, she nods at me. "I'll find a flag," she says.

There is no doubt that building the replica is challenging. The model, the style, the structure is the easy part. Handling the slippery bricks is the hard part. I carry the red pieces in my mouth and place them in the center of the floor. I have no idea how I'm going to snap them all together. For now, I just push them into the shape of a square, three rows on each side, like the three floors of the shelter.

Clementine, in the meantime, hops up onto the kitchen counter. "Hey, look at this," she says, pushing a mug toward the edge, where it teeters like Laverne's fishbowl. "It's filled with colorful flaggy-looking things. They look like umbrellas for hamsters. Fashion accessories for Mo! I'll send it all down to you."

"No! Clementine, you're going to—"

CRASH!

The mug falls on the floor, breaks into pieces, and sends the flaggy-looking hamster umbrellas scattering.

"Shhhhhh!" I say, trying to whisper. But it's too late. Georgina is awake and standing in front of me. She doesn't speak. She just sits down next to me and stares.

I press my head into the palm of her hand and lick at her fingertips. Georgina, I'm counting on you.

Georgina picks up two red bricks, one in each hand. She flips them around between her thumbs and forefingers. She looks at the arrangement on the floor. She looks at me. Then *SNAP!* She presses two together. Then she does it again with two more. *SNAP!* Then two more. *SNAP.* I don't know a more beautiful sound. Soon Georgina is on her hands and knees snapping bricks together faster than I've ever seen.

I look at Clementine, who holds a blue-and-red umbrella flag in her mouth. "Itsh for zzhe top," she says.

I circle around Georgina, headbutting her leg, her hip, her arms. So grateful. So proud. So full of . . . I don't know what I'm full of, but it feels right.

We work together. I nod and nudge and Georgina snaps and snaps, and in no time at all, the shelter replica is done. It is small. Much smaller than the other structures that had taken days and weeks to complete. But there is no doubt in my mind that it is the City Shelter of Care and Comfort.

Georgina motions for Clementine to bring over the flag. I smile at Clementine, who drops the flag into Georgina's hand and comes to sit next to me. With wide eyes and a lump in my throat, I watch Georgina wedge the flag between two bricks on the top of the structure. Then the three of us admire what we've created.

Georgina lifts me into one arm and Clementine into the other and whispers, "I know what you want, Elvis. We'll go in the morning."

Georgina carries us both back to the bed-in-a-sofa. I sit on the back of it and look out at the moonlit sky. The shelter is a silhouette with a glow around it. "Thank you, Georgina," I say. "I love you."

I look at Clementine, and I am surprised at what I feel. "I love you, too, Clementine."

 # Chapter 29

I wake early and jump up onto the back of the sofa to check and make sure the shelter is still there.

Then I jump to the floor and over to the replica. It wasn't a dream. We built it!

Georgina and Clementine soon join me on the floor, and when Daddy comes in, he sits, too.

"Wow, G. Someone was busy last night," he says. "Do I know this structure?"

"Daddy, it's the City Shelter of Care and Comfort," Georgina says. "We built it."

"Yes, you did," Daddy says.

"We're going to the shelter today, Daddy," Georgina says. "Elvis and Clementine, they want to go. And we have to take them."

I wait for Daddy to say something negative. Something about how Georgina must be confused. But instead, he smiles at Georgina and says, "Okay." He gets up and walks into the kitchen. "Are you sure about this?"

"Positive. Can you please find out what time the shelter opens?"

"I can tell this is important to you, Georgina," he says.

"It is."

"You know I'd do anything for Clementine. And Elvis, too." he says. "Come eat some breakfast. Then we'll get dressed and go. Also, why are the fancy drink umbrellas all over the floor?"

Georgina runs over and collects all the little flaggy things.

"I really like Daddy," I say to Clementine.

"Who wouldn't?" she says.

Georgina opens the cardboard carrier, and Clementine and I jump right in, and we walk to the shelter. The air is warm and smells of grass and cars and all the things that exist in the out-of-doors. I watch through the peek holes as the shelter gets closer and closer. Old Glory is at the top, shifting just barely. We walk right through the double doors, and the familiar scent of cats and dogs mixes with the nose-tingling smell of clean. Is there anything better?

No one is at the front desk, so we head straight in. Georgina and Daddy walk us through the shelter, with the felines on one side and the canines on the other. It's just like I remember. I see a volunteer pushing a cart crammed with the usual cleaning supplies and food and water bowls. Georgina stops in front of the glass room with the glass door. It's the Second Chance Club. A poster hangs on the wall.

"There you are," I say to Clementine.

"C'est moi," she says.

"Say what?"

"Oh, for the love of furballs, Elvis. It's me. The poster pet of second chances."

I look down the corridor to the back of the building. "My condo is down there," I say. "The place where Etta and I lived for so long."

My heart squeezes in my chest.

Georgina continues walking around, and we end up back at the front where the adoption desk is. She sets the carrier on the counter. From this perch, I can see the whole place, just like on the day of the Fourth of July Adoption Extravaganza. Across from the desk on the wall is a gigantic poster that says July Fourth. There are letters forming words that I don't know. But I can tell it's a poster from that life-changing day. And whose picture is plastered on the front? It's Rupert. All fluffy and happy. You can even see his eyes. He went to his forever home and was happy about it. And they put him on a poster. Wow!

It feels like just yesterday that I left this place. It really had been my home. Is it still my home? Do I belong here? And what about Etta? The questions whizz around my head and make me dizzy.

I'm not sure how we are going to find out what we came here to find out, and I am suddenly worried. I mew, long and loud. Rupert is on a poster. But Etta isn't.

Someone approaches the desk, but I can't see their face through the peek holes. "Are you returning these cats? We've had a few returns this week."

I dart around and strain my neck. I'd know that voice anywhere.

"No, no," Georgina says. "We got these cats here. Clementine a while ago, and Elvis on the Fourth of July."

"Elvis!"

It's Carly. She opens the carrier and looks in at us. "Hey there, sweet pea. And Clementine! From the poster. Our Second Chance champion."

"Hi, Carly. It's me," I say.

"I know," she says. "I love you, too."

Carly reaches in and scratches behind my ears. She strokes Clementine on her back. She is so kind, but some things never change.

"What can I do for you all?" she says, lifting me out of the carrier and snuggling me like in the old days. I let my motor run for a moment to let her know that I still like her.

"I'm here to help my cats," Georgina says. "Elvis wanted to come. So did Clementine."

"They did? Wow, most of our residents don't want to come back once they've found their forever homes."

"There's something about this shelter that is very important to both of them," Georgina says.

"I understand," Carly says. "I just wish they could speak to us, you know? And tell us exactly what they need."

"I'm speaking now," I say, bringing my motor to an abrupt halt.

"Aww. Elvis is so full of love," Carly says. "Hey, you know we just got a postcard from the couple who adopted Elvis's sister. Let me see if I can find it."

"Elvis has a sister!" Georgina says.

Carly puts me back in the carrier and my heart starts pounding.

"What's a postcard, Clementine?" I say.

"It's like a letter."

"From the alphabet?"

"No. The kind that comes in the mail."

"Oh, right," I say, not that I have any idea what that means. "But a couple adopted Etta!" I let that sink in for a moment. Etta was adopted.

"Elvis wants to see his family," Georgina says. My heart swoons. She knows.

Daddy doesn't say a word. But he seems to be lending emotional support, like Mo.

I sit at full attention while Georgina sticks her fingers in the peek holes of the carrier. Clementine busies herself with grooming her orange patch.

Carly is back in a flash, her arms swinging around her body. "I got it!" she says, waving something in the air.

"I can't believe this, Clementine. A postcard from Etta," I say. "Mo is never going to believe this. That we made our way to the shelter. He's going to flip. Probably a standing backflip! The postcard has an address, right? With a zip code. Maybe Etta lives in 94611 like us."

"Elvis," Clementine says, "it's true that Mo will be happy. But let's take it easy."

Carly holds the postcard in both hands. It is small, and I can see that it has lots of letters on it. Carly reads it.

Dear Carly,
Just a quick hello and kitten update. Etta is happy at her new home. She's settled in quite well and has grown so much. She loves to curl up in Jonathan's sock drawer and purr. Her motor sure is something. We are so happy and grateful for the opportunity to be a family. Thank you to the City Shelter of Care and Comfort. We love Etta so much!

All the best,
Jonathan and Evan Burton-Lee

City
809
Oak

"Isn't it wonderful, Elvis?" Carly says. "Your sister is so happy with her forever family. They live in San Jose.

Now let's take a picture and I'll send it back to the Burton-Lees. Won't that be nice?"

"Is San Jose in our zip code?" I say. "94611?"

"I don't think so," Clementine says.

This isn't what I thought would happen. I thought I would find out more. I thought I would get to see Etta. Or something.

"San Jose is kind of far away," Georgina says softly. She looks at me through the peek holes. "I think you miss your sister," she says. "Elvis and Etta." Georgina looks back at Daddy. "There were two of them."

"Yes, so there were." Daddy puts his arm around Georgina.

Where is San Jose?

"It's perfect," Carly says. "All we ever hope for is that our animals are happy and well cared for. The Burton-Lees are wonderful. It's a best-case scenario. How about a picture of the four of you now?"

Georgina lifts me out of the carrier. I can hardly breathe. My eyes dart around, looking for signs of Etta. San Jose? I look at Clementine cuddled in Daddy's arms.

"You're going to be fine," Clementine says.

I think of Etta's gray fluff. Her little white paws.

I think of us together. Listening to Carly's stories.

Pretending to be *X*es. The snuggling. The treading. Our life. The one that used to be.

"Smile, Elvis," Clementine says. "Smile for Etta."

A light flashes.

The Burton-Lees. Jonathan's sock drawer. Etta's forever home.

I blink.

My eyes sting.

I feel dizzy.

And sick.

"You make a beautiful family," Carly says.

 # Chapter 30

I settle back in the carrier with Clementine and stare out the peek holes.

Etta is happy and safe. That is all I should hope for. But I feel empty. And lost.

"I'm sorry, Elvis," Clementine says. She presses her face into mine. "I was rooting for you. I really was. But at least you have answers."

I try my best to focus on the positive.

"Clementine," Georgina says. "We need to find out about Clementine. Maybe she has a sister, too."

Daddy speaks up. "I adopted her last fall, just before Halloween. She was such a sad little gal. So scrawny. Her fur was matted and thin. But I loved her immediately. And look at her now. Healthy and beautiful!"

I look at Clementine, who is hanging on Daddy's every word.

"Can we find out if she had relatives?" Georgina says. "You know, littermates. Like Elvis."

Why is it that every time someone says my name, my heart pounds out of my chest?

"Oh, I didn't start working here until May," Carly says. "I only know Clementine from her poster."

"Yeah. I figured it was a long shot," Daddy says. "I'm sorry, Georgina."

"But I can look in her file and see what I can find. Last October, right? Give me a couple minutes."

Clementine looks at me with wide eyes, but then she closes them and goes back to licking her orange patch. I press my eyes to the peek holes. I can't see where Carly has gone. "Maybe she'll find some information," I say.

"It's not likely," Clementine says.

But Carly comes right back with papers in her hands and a smile on her face. "She didn't have a littermate. But she had kittens. Four of them," she says.

"Four kittens!" Georgina says.

Clementine stops preening and looks at me with a blank expression.

"We keep pretty good files here. All four were adopted. Two of them went together to a nice family up north. One went to San Francisco—looks like Nob

Hill—fancy! And the fourth. He was adopted, too. And of all the luck. He came back to us a couple weeks ago. He's been in the back room, with the veterinarians, until just yesterday. Honestly, it's a miracle that you're here today."

Clementine stands up. "Elvis," she says. "Oh, Elvis." She looks at me, and I think she might faint. I think *I* might faint!

Carly opens the carrier again. She reaches in and holds Clementine's face in her hands. "Your kitten is in the Second Chance Club right this minute."

Everything that happens next happens so fast that it is a blur. Georgina picks up the carrier and practically runs all of us over to the glass doors of the Second Chance Club. Looking through the peek holes is not easy. I keep getting knocked around. Carly opens the doors and Georgina steps in and sets the carrier on the floor.

"Elvis and Clementine must stay in the carrier. Policy," Carly says.

I have a decent view of the place and try to spot Clementine's kitten. "Can you see this, Clementine?" I say. "Are you seeing this?"

"Yes," she says softly.

Carly kneels on the floor. "Eliot. Eliot. Come on out. There's someone here to see you."

I spot the gray tip of a slim tail curled around the carpeted scratching post in a corner of the room. Very slowly, a white paw reaches out, followed by another. Then the whole body of a fluffy feline.

"Oh, Daddy," Georgina says, squatting down next to Carly. "Eliot."

Clementine practically pushes her whole self through a peek hole. "That's my boy," she says. "That's my Eliot." A short, high-pitched mew escapes her mouth. I nudge up against her.

"That's your Eliot," I say.

Eliot creeps over to Carly, and she pulls him into her arms. "He's shy and skittish. And he wasn't good with people for quite a while, but I've managed to befriend him."

"What happened to him?" Georgina asks.

"We don't know for sure. Only that his owner said he went missing for a few days, and when he showed up again, he was weak and scared. He could have been hit by a car. Who knows? But then the owner had to move and felt it best to bring him back. It's unfortunate."

"It's not unfortunate for Clementine," Daddy says. "This is amazing."

Clementine calls for him. "Eliot. Eliot."

Eliot looks over at us.

"He knows you," I say.

Eliot jumps from Carly's arms and comes right over to our carrier. He peers through a peek hole.

"Eliot," Clementine says again.

"I know you," Eliot says.

"Yes," Clementine replies.

"You're my mother."

What happens next fills a part of the emptiness in my heart.

Eliot coos.

Clementine glows.

Georgina begs.

Daddy stammers.

Carly keeps saying how much she loves us all.

And before you can say "holy habitat," there is a third cat in our cardboard carrier. It's not Etta. But seeing Clementine with one of her kittens saves my life in a way that I cannot explain.

After a few moments back at the adoption desk, and for the second time in my life, I watch through the peek holes as the magnificent red bricks, the sparkling glass windows, and Old Glory—swaying in the breeze at the top of the City Shelter of Care and Comfort—fade from my view.

Saturday, September 4, 11:43 AM

Mommy!

Thank you for finding the album and the picture.

Look what we got!

Daddy just texted.

He's beautiful, Georgina.

You're going to love him! 🐱 🖤 🐾 💕

 # Chapter 31

I don't speak at all in the carrier.

Clementine preens and cleans her boy and her boy turns on the loudest motor that I've ever heard. It all seems as unlikely as a man walking a tightrope between two towers a thousand feet in the sky.

They wouldn't be together if we hadn't built the replica of the shelter. And that wouldn't have happened if we hadn't gone to Daddy's for the weekend. And we wouldn't have gone to Daddy's for the weekend if Georgina hadn't asked to bring me. And Georgina wouldn't have asked to bring me if I didn't live in her bedroom. And I wouldn't live in her bedroom if Mo wasn't so nice and if I hadn't tried to leave and hurt my leg and accidentally knocked over Laverne's bowl and gotten mad at Bambi and . . .

I close my eyes.

Clementine wouldn't be with Eliot if I hadn't tried to find Etta.

Etta.

You're with the Burton-Lees. In San Jose. At your forever home with your forever family. But you're still my sister.

I love you, Etta. I will never forget you.

"Mommy and I had a quick text chat," Daddy says. "She agrees that it is best if we all go back to her house. The apartment rules and all."

"No cats allowed is really stupid," Georgina says.

I couldn't agree more.

"I'll stay for the day, G, and help Eliot get adjusted," Daddy says.

"Yay!" Georgina says. She sticks her fingers through the peek holes. "I'm sorry you didn't get to see your sister, Elvis," she says. "But you are here with me. With all of us. And we love you so much."

I close my eyes and sigh. Daddy's rambling contraption of a car hits a bump in the road and Eliot and Clementine fall right on top of me, squishing me into the side of the carrier. They laugh. I laugh, too. There are so many emotions, but one thing is sure. I cannot wait to tell Mo everything that has happened.

"You know, G," Daddy says. "I've been thinking about it. Maybe it's time for a bigger apartment. One that allows pets."

When we arrive at home, Mommy is standing on the front porch. She shakes her head. But then she smiles with all her teeth. "Three cats," she says. "I guess this is our new normal."

"Mommy, it's so exciting! Eliot is Clementine's kitten. He's almost full-grown, and he's so cute. Clementine is so happy. We just had to get him. Daddy's going to move to a bigger apartment so he can have pets, and then Elvis and Clementine and Eliot can go with me when I go to Daddy's. It's all perfect!"

"Oh my goodness," Mommy says.

"And Elvis has a sister, Mommy. A sister. She lives in San Jose!" Georgina dances around all of us, and, honestly, you'd have to be a real party pooper not to celebrate.

"Georgina is right, Vanessa," Daddy says. And my first thought is, who's Vanessa? But then I figure it out. Of course I figure it out. I'm not stupid. "I couldn't possibly leave Eliot at the shelter."

"I know," Mommy/Mrs. Pemberton/Vanessa says. Then she hands Georgina a small book, opened to a page with pictures. Georgina looks at it for a long time.

"It was on the bookshelf all along," Mommy says.

I watch Georgina fiddle with a plastic covering of sorts and gently take a picture out of the album. She studies it closely and then looks at Mommy. "Thank you, Mommy," she says.

Mommy reaches down and holds Georgina's face in her hands, and for the first time, I watch Georgina put her arms around her mother.

"I love you, Georgina," Mommy says.

"We both do," Daddy says.

"I love you, too."

Chapter 32

Clementine gets right to the business of showing Eliot around the house, and I beeline up to our room in search of Mo.

Laverne splashes out her warning. "INCOMING! ELVIS!"

I must admit that I love when Laverne shouts my name.

Mo is sitting on the top of his plastic palace, working on his trap door or something. "I thought you were staying at Daddy's for the whole weekend," he says.

"We came home early. There is so much to tell you, Mo."

"I'm glad you're back. Tell me everything!"

Mo climbs down onto the floor and comes and sits in front of me. I start at the beginning, when we arrived at Daddy's. How his house is near the shelter. How I came up with a plan. How we built the City Shelter of Care and Comfort. And all the rest.

"I'm sorry that you didn't get to see Etta," he says. "But, Elvis. What you did. It's marvelous."

"Georgina understood me, Mo. She knew what I was saying. You were right. It was like magic. And then we heard about Etta. And we found Eliot."

"It's a world of wonder," Mo says.

Clementine comes into the room, beaming with pride. "I can never repay you, Elvis," she says. She strides over to Mo, so proud, with Eliot at her side. "Mo, I'd like to introduce you to my son. This is Eliot."

"Hello, young man," Mo says.

"Hello," Eliot says.

"Eliot, you might feel a certain urge in your tummy regarding Mo," Clementine says. "But please ignore it. We are family."

"Yes, mother."

Clementine brings Eliot over to meet Laverne, and naturally she flips and shouts, "ELIOT!"

Pretty soon everyone is in Georgina's room, including Mommy and Daddy.

"Full house," Mommy says.

"That's the way I like it," Georgina says.

I jump up onto Georgina's bed and settle in the place where I can see everything. And just as expected, Georgina dumps out a bin of LEGOs and opens *The Big Book of American Architecture*.

"Daddy, you have to stay for a little while longer," Georgina says. "I've decided what we're making next."

"Oh, tell me," Daddy says, sitting on the floor and grabbing a few bricks.

Mo trickles over to Georgina and nibbles at her fingertips. Then he scampers in circles when she finds the page she's looking for. "The Freedom Tower!" she says.

"I should have guessed that," Daddy says.

Mommy sits on the floor, too. "You know, Georgina," she says. "There was a time I thought I might become an architect."

"I know, Mommy. But you decided to work for a bank instead. I've heard this before."

"The Freedom Tower has such an interesting design," Mommy says. "It will be tricky to build."

Georgina nods at Mommy. "I accept the challenge."

"We didn't do anything like this at my other house," Eliot says.

Clementine and Eliot find a cozy space to snuggle, right next to me, on the foot of Georgina's bed.

"I hope you'll tell me about your other house," Clementine says. "When you're ready."

"I will, Mother," he says.

Mommy, Daddy, and Georgina sit on the floor and begin snapping bricks. They talk about the Twin Towers. About never forgetting. And honoring those who lost their lives. And all who suffered. I still don't understand why someone would fly an airplane into a skyscraper. Mo says that sometimes in life the information we want is not available to us. He must be right. I don't know who lost their lives. But when I think about those who have suffered, I'm pretty sure they mean everyone. In the whole world.

"I'm glad that whoever made the decision to rebuild the World Trade Center decided to do it," Georgina says.

"Georgina," Mommy says. "Daddy and I have discussed it, and I'd like to take you to New York City for Christmas. There is so much to see and so much to learn."

Georgina's eyes light up.

"It will be a Christmas present, from both of us," Daddy says.

I see smiles. And water-filled eyes.

Daddy talks about how he is going to find a new apartment, one that accepts pets. Georgina says she'll

bring all of us with her when she goes to Daddy's. Mommy says that doesn't sound normal. Georgina tells her it will be perfectly fine. The three of them snap brick after brick. *SNAP, SNAP.* Mo is there, too. His delicate fingers, sorting and stacking. I marvel, again, at the way in which Mo presents each brick—a precious gift—to Georgina. All of this gives me a feeling that I can't quite describe. Each *SNAP* sounds like the broken pieces of life fitting back together, like they are meant to be.

Soon, the weight of my eyelids pulls down over my eyes. I try to keep them open, but instead, I let the foggy fuzz of slumber settle in.

As I drift off, I think of Etta. I imagine her with the Burton-Lees at her forever home in San Jose. She looks just like herself. She is comfortable. Warm. I can see her, in my mind's eye, cuddled up in that sock drawer, her little white paws treading in her sleep. Her motor is on. It's a soft, content rumble. I feel it all around me. The best feeling in the world.

Chapter 33

After a very busy weekend, the Freedom Tower is done, and it's standing right next to the Twin Towers. It's slightly taller than the Twins. Georgina already told us that the real one is 1,776 feet tall. The spire at the top makes it the tallest in the United States. It's a beauty.

I look up at the tip-top and laugh. "Mo, what are you doing up there?"

"Elvis, this thing is marvelous."

"How did I know you were going to say that?"

"Do you see how the sides are like facets of a diamond? They're actually isosceles triangles. Eight of them!"

"Of course they are," I say, not having ever heard some of those words before.

Mo trickles down the side and scurries right up to my face, and all I can think is, *Here we go again.*

"Okay," I say. "Let's get this over with. Tell me who the architect is."

"David Childs!"

"And the amazing and useless fact you can't wait to reveal?"

"Okay. I'm so glad you asked. You know how Georgina told us the Freedom Tower is 1,776 feet tall—the tallest building in the country?"

"Yes."

"Well, the height is a tribute to the year our country was founded—1776! That's when the Declaration of Independence was signed."

"The Declaration of Independence? Like, Independence Day? Like, the Fourth of July?"

"Yes! Exactly."

"Wow!" I say. Who would have thought? A fact that is not entirely useless. I let the notion settle into my brain.

1776.

The Fourth of July Adoption Extravaganza.

Me and Etta.

Carly. Mrs. Pemberton. Mo. Laverne. Clementine. Georgina. Skyscrapers. Daddy. The City Shelter of Care and Comfort. The Burton-Lees. Eliot. My head is spinning.

"I'm pretty sure everything in the whole world is connected," I say.

"I'm glad you finally figured that out," Mo says. "We're all in it together."

"Sometimes the crowd is overwhelming," Clementine says from the doorway.

"I love it," Eliot says. "I never knew I could be connected to a skyscraper."

"INCOMING! THE KID!"

Georgina plops down right next to us. "School starts tomorrow. Today is the last day of summer vacation," she says with a sigh. That reminds me that I don't even know what day today is.

While Georgina cleans up a few stray bricks, I hustle out to the hallway to check the calendar.

"It's Monday, September 6," I say to Mo.

"Yes, it is. Labor Day!"

"What the heck is that?" I say.

"It's a national holiday. A day to honor those who work hard," he says.

"Like the people who built the skyscrapers?"

"Exactly!"

Mo would know. I've never met anyone who works as hard as he does.

I watch Georgina lift the Freedom Tower up to her shelf. She puts the Twins right next to it. Then she places the picture—the one from the album—in front of them. She takes a nice long look at the photo and turns to us.

She looks proud of her work.

Mo is proud, too.

And so am I.

Mommy and Daddy

We talked about 9/11 today.

I showed Ms. Doyle pictures of my skyscrapers.

She asked me to show the whole class.

She said my skyscrapers are an important tribute.

Can I invite a friend over this weekend?

Daddy

G, That's wonderful.

Mommy

Yes, yes to the friend!

Let's talk about it when you get home.

Please only use this phone for emergencies.

I know. ❤

 # Chapter 34

On the afternoon of Saturday, September 11, the doorbell rings, and Georgina rushes out of our room and bounds down the stairs.

When she comes back, we are all surprised.

"It's another human girl," I say to Mo.

"It certainly is," he says.

The girl bounces into our room right behind Georgina. She looks like the human girls that I used to see at the shelter. Hair falling all around her face, shiny white teeth, happy bursts spilling out all over the place.

"I love your room!" she says. "Oh my gosh, your pets! There are so many. Is that a hamster?"

"Yes, that's Mo. And this is Elvis, and over there is Clementine and Eliot, and I have a goldfish, too. This is Laverne. Everyone, this is my new friend, Marisol."

Marisol's eyes dart back and forth between all of us. I'm not sure what her next move will be, and I prepare to scoot under the bed if necessary.

"Look at all your skyscrapers," Marisol says. Then a chatter-fest starts. They talk about buildings and towers and architects and LEGOs. LEGO this. LEGO that. I never knew there could be so much to say about little plastic bricks.

My whiskers twitch, my tail snaps, and I don't know exactly why, but I let out a yowl. A questioning yowl. I look over at Mo.

"Georgina has a new friend," he says. "We need to be happy for her."

"I'm happy for her," Eliot says. "We never had any human girls at my old house."

Clementine gently nudges her son.

"Of course I'm happy," I say. Please. It's right and good for Georgina to have a human friend. But I feel a tap on my heart. A pluck. A tiny sting.

"You are really good at building skyscrapers," Marisol says. "Do you like bridges? I'm thinking about building the Golden Gate Bridge."

"It was built in 1937," Georgina says.

"I know," Marisol says. "It took four years to build."

"I know," Georgina says. "Did you know that even though it looks red, the color is—"

"International Orange! I know."

Georgina grabs Marisol by the elbow. "Follow me," she says. "You're gonna love this."

The two girls climb out the window. I know exactly where Georgina is taking Marisol, and I know exactly what they'll see. I think about following but change my mind and jump up onto the foot of Georgina's bed.

I glance over at Eliot and Clementine, a couple of furballs twisted and tangled together.

Mo climbs up there, too, scurries over to me, and reaches out to hold my cheeks. Such a hamster!

"We need to be on standby, Elvis," he says.

"Oh, yeah?" I say.

"Yes. I have a suspicion that Georgina and Marisol are going to start a new project. And if they need our help, we need to be ready."

"You know, Mo. I really like helping," I say. "I think it might be my raisin thing."

"Your raisin thing?" Mo reaches out to grab a whisker. "Oh, you mean your *raison d'être*. Your purpose. Ha! Well, there is no greater purpose than helping another."

"We're a team, aren't we, Mo?" I say.

"Yes, we are," he says. "Always."

Mo trickles up my foreleg and makes his way to his spot at the nape of my neck. His hamster nails tickle, and a shiver spreads all the way to the tip of my tail. A breeze comes through the open window. Cool. Fresh. Mo tugs on my ear, and I let out another yowl. The good kind. The satisfying kind. The kind that makes me think about bridges and friends.

Georgina and Marisol climb back through the window, both of them smiling. They lean into each other and wrinkle their noses and giggle. Humans! They're so silly.

In the middle of the room, Georgina and Marisol dump out a bin of LEGOs and start sorting. Suddenly, I see it. The rainbow. The sunlight streams through the window and lands like a pot of gold right between Georgina and Marisol.

I set my head on my paws and wrap my tail around my body and whisper to Mo, "The best room in the house."

"Isn't it marvelous?" Mo says.

"Yes, it is," I say.

Then I close my eyes and turn on my motor.

It's the perfect time for an afternoon nap.

Author's Note

On September 11, 2001, at 8:46 A.M. Eastern Daylight Time, hijacked American Airlines Flight 11 flew into the North Tower of the World Trade Center in New York City, hitting floors 94 through 99. Seventeen minutes later, United Airlines Flight 175 hit the South Tower. Because these airplanes were scheduled to fly all the way to Los Angeles, they carried nearly twenty thousand gallons of gasoline each. After impact, fire took over, and the insides of the towers reached two thousand degrees Fahrenheit. The steel columns of the structures melted. By 10:30 A.M., both towers had collapsed. The world struggled to understand.

9/11 is one of many tragic events in history. For some, it feels like a story—something that happened long ago. It will surely be studied and discussed for years to come, and we will never forget the hurt inflicted, the lives lost, and the unfair blaming. And yet, other types of tragedies, large and small, will continue to occur. Sheltermates will be separated. Parents will get divorced. Nations will feud. Plans will change.

Whatever the tragedy, the one thing that those experiencing loss have in common is the necessity to move forward. At the time of this writing, the world is in lockdown due to COVID-19, and we are all struggling to find that new way forward.

In writing Elvis's story, I wanted to explore the idea of rebuilding in the face of devastation, from a simple LEGO project to a New York skyscraper. From a home to a family to a new way of life. In 2001, at the time that 9/11 shook us all to the core, I was in the midst of struggling to find a way to rebuild my own life. It was a grand undertaking that required, as Mo would say, resilience and fortitude. I believe that we all inherently possess these qualities, and we are called to use them, sometimes as a family, sometimes as a nation, sometimes as an entire world, but always as individuals—and that includes animals, of course! In many ways, this book is the culmination of my own rebuilding. I hope it inspires you to move forward with whatever it is that must be rebuilt.

For more information on 9/11, visit the 9/11 Memorial & Museum at 911memorial.org.

Acknowledgments

It's a modern-day miracle!!!

This is what it feels like to write, revise, revise again (and again), sell, and publish a book! How on earth does anyone do it? With a little help from your friends, of course.

I want to thank, first and foremost, my very first creative writing instructors from the writing programs at UC Berkeley Extension. Monica Wesolowska critiqued my first-ever manuscript and pointed out my strengths. Laurie Ann Doyle looked me in the eye and said, "Lisa, honor your gift." Without these encouraging teachers, I might never have moved forward with my writing.

A hearty thank-you to EVERYONE at Hamline University's MFAC program. Thank you to Mary Rockcastle, my four stellar semester advisors, Jackie Briggs Martin, Laurel Snyder, Phyllis Root, and Eliot Schrefer, and all the amazing faculty who brought their best each and every semester. Special praise to my workshop leaders: Elana K. Arnold, Swati Avasthi, Lisa Jahn-Clough, Nina LaCour, Marsha Qualey, Claire Rudolf Murphy,

Anne Ursu, and Marsha Wilson Chall. A huge hug to my cohort, the Quadropus, for all the support, advice, late-night talks, early morning coffees, and all-around brilliance: Ben Cromwell, Katie Dunlop, Markelle Grabo, Emily Hill, Jessica Kieran, Kalena Miller, Trisha Parsons, Tom Sebanc, Elizabeth Selin, Ari Tison, Jonathan Van Gieson, Sarah Wilson Rickman (Sarah, you were right), and Kerry Xiong.

A huge shout-out to my other amazing critique partners who have nudged me forward: Pamela Berkman, Joanna Ho, Tina Hoggatt, Laura King, Louis Lafair, Lily LaMotte, Kirsten Pendreigh, and L. M. Quraishi. Extra-special gratitude to Aimee Lucido for holding my hand throughout the whole process! Some critique partners come in the form of your fourth-grade niece. Thank you, Charlotte Frenkel—what a difference one word makes. Some writing partners start with an eye for craft and end up as one of your dearest friends. I could not have done this without you, Cyn Nooney. If you have a family member who is highly intelligent, is willing to read all your work, and can also give you meaningful feedback, you are lucky indeed. For me, that person is my daughter, Julia Ormond. I can't thank you enough, Julia. I am so impressed with you.

Love and gratitude go out to all of the staff and animals at the East Bay SPCA, where Julia and I spent seven years volunteering in the feline department. We would have adopted all of you. But, alas, we had a full house already with Juliet, Samantha, Missy, Hannah, Charcoal, and the unforgettable and real-life Mo.

I want to thank my lovely and wise agent, Jennifer Mattson, for noticing my work and seeing the possibilities. I am so grateful to be working with you, Jennifer. Thank you to my editor, Erica Finkel, for adopting Elvis and taking such good care of this book. Special thanks to everyone at Amulet Books, especially Emily Daluga, Megan Carlson, Kathy Lovisolo, Jade Rector, and Andrew Smith. Thank you to Olivia Chin Mueller for bringing Elvis and his entire world to life with your brilliant illustrations.

Thank you Juliana Jones-Munson and the Funsons (often thought to be a popular rock band!) for helping me embrace the me in me. And finally, thank you to my family, all of the Frenkels, the Ormonds, and the Riddioughs. To my parents, Robert and Elizabeth Frenkel, and my siblings, Laura Williams and Rob Frenkel, for steadfast support and excitement around not just my writing, but my entire life. To Pat Riddiough, for loving everything I write. To Andrea Carpenter, for listening to my never-ending babble. To my son, James Ormond, for being a brilliant example of fortitude and resilience. Again, to my daughter, Julia Ormond, for all of everything. And to Jim Riddiough: You've given me time, space, encouragement, and love, and presented these things to me like the precious gifts they are. It's a world of wonder, and I'm lucky enough to get to live in it!

About the Author

Lisa Frenkel Riddiough is a Northern California-based writer who earned her MFA in Writing for Children and Young Adults from Hamline University. She is a former sales executive, an avid squirrel watcher, a frequent baker of chocolate pound cake, and an exclamation point enthusiast! *Elvis and the World As It Stands* is her debut novel!! Learn more about Lisa at www.lisariddiough.com.